DON'T GIVE A DAMN ABOUT MY PLAID REPUTATION

CAROLINE LEE

ABOUT THIS BOOK

Lady Robena Oliphant loves two things in life: her piping and Laird Kester MacBain. Unfortunately, it seems she is destined to have neither. The prestigious piping competition at the Highland Games is open only to men...and Kester has conveniently forgotten to mention he's betrothed to someone else. The jerk.

Well, she might not be able to do anything about her broken heart, but perhaps 'tis time she found a way to share her music with the world. All she has to do is cut her hair and don a lad's kilt....

To end a long-standing feud, the King has ordered Kester to journey to the Highland Games and marry the daughter of his enemy. His heart—and other bits—ache at the thought of giving up his precious Robena, but an honorable laird must follow his King's commands. When the MacBains are joined on their journey by a curious lad with beautiful eyes Kester knows only too well, and the world's most unlikely mustache, he's flabbergasted. How do his men not see "Robbie" as the beauty she really is? This journey just got more interesting, if *uncomfortable* in the kilt department.

Unfortunately, the Games—which mark the end of their time together—loom ever closer. Kester *must* marry another. But if Robena is brave enough to put her reputation on the line, might she win both her music and a future with the man she loves?

Warning: medieval road-trip romance has never been funnier! As with all of Caroline's HistRomComs, get ready for hilarious anachronisms, plenty of dirty jokes, and steamy scenes hot enough to need a fan! You're in for a lot of fun!

The Sweet Cheyenne Quartet (6 books)

Sweet Contemporary Westerns
    Quinn Valley Ranch (5 books)
    River's End Ranch (14 books)
    The Cowboys of Cauldron Valley (7 books)
    The Calendar Girls' Ranch (6 books)

Click **here** to find a complete list of Caroline's books.

*Sign up for Caroline's Newsletter to receive exclusive content and freebies, as well as first dibs on her books! Or if newsletters aren't your thing, follow her on **Bookbub** for a quick, concise new release alert every time she publishes a book!*

CHAPTER 1

THIS KISS, like the one before, and the one before that, tasted of *perfection*.

Their lips—their very souls—melded in a melody unlike any she'd ever experienced, the notes plucking at her heart… and lower. She squirmed against his hardness, feeling like a taut lute string waiting to be strummed by a master.

Robena Oliphant had known the moment she'd set eyes on him that Kester MacBain was the man—the warrior, the fallen angel!—for her. Although he'd tried to be honorable, she'd finally worn him down.

And now…!

When his teeth caught her lower lip and tugged slightly, she didn't bother to swallow down the moan that rolled from her chest. In fact, she leaned closer, rubbing that chest against his.

St. Kelsi bless her, but Kester could *kiss*.

Because he was so much taller than her, she had to content herself with wrapping her arms around his waist, locking her fingers together behind him as if she could lock him similarly in place.

She didn't want him going anywhere.

Not now, not *ever*.

He'd already taught her what to do with her tongue, and Robena showed that she'd been an eager student, wrenching a groan from him as he pushed forward. Her back rubbed against the stone of the corridor wall, his palms on either side of her head.

She was trapped—exactly where she wanted to be.

Stuck between a wall and—if that persistent stiffness poking into her navel was any indication—a hard place.

Her lips curled upward against his.

With a muttered curse, he dragged his lips away from hers and she beamed up at him as he straightened.

"Thank ye, sir, may I have another?" 'Twas what she'd said not ten minutes ago, which had led to him pushing her up against the wall in this hidden corridor and kissing her.

Mayhap 'twould work again.

But….

"Robena, damnation."

Instead of lowering his lips to hers once more, he blew out a breath and she was a little alarmed to realize it sounded frustrated.

She tightened her hold on his waist. "Come along, Kester. My sister's wedding celebration isnae for hours yet, and 'tis far too busy out there in the great hall. Are ye no' glad I offered to give ye a tour of the secret passages?"

The way his lips curled upward seemed almost reluctant. And he sighed again.

"Aye, I confess I've been curious about them since we arrived." He lifted one palm from the wall to scrub across his face, so his next words were muffled. "Even if I could guess what would happen if I let ye drag me off alone."

She grinned unrepentantly, thinking of their careful dance in the last weeks. "'Twas no' so bad, was it?" Her hips flexed against his, silently reminding him of the pleasure he'd just shown her.

Kissing Kester MacBain had been just as wonderful as she'd known it would be.

But he shook his head. And when he flattened his palm against the wall by her face, he seemed…dejected.

"Lass, I cannae deny kissing ye was…."

When he trailed off, she tried to tamp down the growing alarm with flippancy. "Bliss? Pleasure beyond yer wildest imaginings?"

His lips curled ruefully. "Aye—well, och, nay. I have some fairly wild imaginings."

Oh good, *here* was the charmer she'd fallen in love with. "I cannae wait to hear all about them."

Her blood was still humming, her skin still tingling from his kisses. Aye, her body was pressed against his, held in place by her locked hands. But otherwise, it had only been their lips touching…and still her nipples were hard peaks straining toward him, and her core *ached* for his touch….

Sometimes, 'tis a burden to have sisters who's taught ye so much about what passes between a man and a woman.

She was ready to learn all she could from Kester.

"I'll no' be sharing them with ye."

Robena blinked. "What?"

"My wildest imaginings." His blue eyes were serious again as they stared down at her. "I'll no' be sharing them with ye."

She rolled her eyes dismissively. "I've learned ye're a modest man, Laird MacBain. I mean, 'tis possible ye've just been oblivious to my attempts to seduce ye—"

"I've been aware, lass." His voice deepened as he dropped his chin but held her gaze. "A man would have to be an idiot to miss the way a beautiful woman like ye threw herself at him."

He thought she was beautiful? The unexpected compliment—or was it a lie?—flustered her, and she shook her head.

"And ye're no' an idiot. So, aye, I've been flirting with ye, and ye've been a gentleman."

Too much of a gentleman, if ye ask me. What's wrong with a little harmless flirting and kissing in hidden corridors?

He closed his eyes on a wince. "Which is why I shouldnae have accepted this tour from ye, even if 'twas fascinating to see how the walls of the main floor of the castle are honeycombed with passages."

"See? Ye're modest."

His eyes flew open. "Modest?"

"Look, I'm no' judging ye." For fun, she flexed her hips forward again, and aye, there was the evidence of his arousal. *Just checking.* "I understand if ye're saving yerself for marriage—"

His choking sound interrupted her, but she shrugged and continued.

"And while I'm no' exactly—"

Now it sounded as if he were dying. Or possibly laughing at her.

"—I *am* saving myself for the man I'm *going* to marry. Ye ken my father has decreed all of us—myself and my five sisters—marry? Whomever marries and produces a grandson first, her husband gets to be the next Oliphant laird, which is frankly stupid. And sexist."

"Sexist?" He sounded as if he were being strangled. Maybe he *was* choking on something.

"Aye, 'tis a word Wynda uses a lot. Ye ken she's always reading something or other. Sexist. It means…." Well, actually, she didn't know, but she could guess. "The most sexy."

"*Sexy?*"

He was adorable, even when he was choking. "Goodness, ye *are* sheltered, are ye no'?" She grinned up at him. "I could help ye with that. I'll share my wildest imaginings with *ye*, if ye share yers with me."

Well, at least he seemed to understand *that* request. He swallowed.

"I told ye lass, I cannae. I *willnae.*"

Robena tucked her fingers into his belt—the one which held his mighty sword and matching dagger—and hid her triumphant smirk when he shuddered. She *knew* he was attracted to her, and she *knew* he enjoyed spending time with her; the last weeks of laughter and fun had proved that.

So why was he playing coy now when it came to the kissing?

"And *I* told *ye* I understand, Kester," she said gently. "If ye want to wait until after we're married, I understand."

Da said they had to be married, and from the moment this Highland laird and his men had arrived at her family's keep weeks ago, she'd known Kester MacBain was the one.

To her surprise, instead of grinning, instead of gently lowering his lips to hers once more, he pushed away from the wall. Since her arms were still locked around him, she went with him, stumbling forward until she unlaced her fingers out of desperation to stay upright. Her hands landed on his hips as he ran both hands through his close-cropped brown hair.

"Lass, I'm no' going to marry ye."

She blinked. "What?"

"I'm no' going to marry ye."

She blinked again.

The words individually made sense. *I'm* was of course a contraction of *I am*. And *going to marry ye,* well that was obvious. She'd been saying them to herself for weeks now.

'Twas the *no'* which was giving her brain some trouble.

"Ye're…*no'* going to marry me?"

His lovely eyes were full of sadness as he dropped his hands to her shoulders, holding her like…like…like a younger sister or something. "Aye, Robena. I cannae marry ye."

Damnation. She'd heard him correctly.

Her heart, which had been a bit afraid to beat for the last moments, decided 'twas a brilliant point to make up for lost time and began to beat double time.

"Cannae?" she whispered.

He bit back a sigh but held her gaze, as if determined to give her that much. "Lass, I've tried no' to give ye false hope these last weeks. I want ye, aye, but I cannae have ye, and ye didnae deserve to be led along by an arsehole like me. Ye're a beautiful woman—"

"Ye dinnae have to lie," she choked out, blinking up at him, uncertain what either of them was actually saying.

"Ye're a beautiful woman," he repeated, his fingers flexing just slightly, digging into her skin beneath the silk of her yellow gown. "And I'd be honored to court ye, and fall in love with ye, and marry someone as talented, as witty, as *caring* as ye are."

She opened her mouth to cry, *So why will ye no'?* but no sound came out. Her throat was dry, and her lips—still delightfully bruised by his kisses—opened and closed. Why wasn't her voice working? She was a singer, a musician; she *depended* on her voice.

"But I cannae," he repeated, his own voice dropping to a whisper.

His eyes flicked between hers, his gaze somehow…*sad.*

He was sad?

She swallowed twice before she was able to rasp out, "Are ye breaking up with me, Kester?"

In a flash, his palms were on her cheeks, and he was holding her face close to his. "Breaking ye? Lass, I would *never* hurt ye—"

"Then what do ye think ye're doing—"

She wrenched her face out of his hold, angry at him and at herself, and of *course* slammed the back of her head against the wall behind her.

When she finished with a groan, he was there.

Despite his words, despite the way he'd just mocked her heart and her declaration, Kester was there for her. He stepped forward, trapping her once more with his body—and cupping the back of her head with his palm. Moments ago she'd been so happy to be here, and now she just wanted to push him away and run and hide.

"Let me see, lass," he murmured, pulling her forward so her nose pressed against his chest. "Does this hurt?"

Although he was likely referring to the way his fingers were prodding at the tenderness on the back of her head, Robena's muffled "Aye" was a response to how good—and how horrible!—it felt to be pressed against him when he'd just made it very clear she couldn't have him.

She felt him sigh again. His breath ruffled her hair and his fingers stilled. He seemed content to just stand there.

Holding her.

And she…well, she was *angry*. Angry at him for making such ridiculous statements. Angry at herself for still loving the way it felt to be held in his arms.

Then, to her surprise, he grunted and shifted forward, pressing her more tightly against the wall. She wasn't certain what to do with her hands, so she curled them into fists in her gown—the gown she'd chosen to wear to her sister's wedding celebration—and tried to hate him.

It didn't work.

"Robena?" His voice sounded strangled.

She didn't want to give him the satisfaction of answering.

"Robena, lass, who else kens we're down here?"

"Nae one," she snapped, her words muffled by his shirt and the plaid he wore across his heart. "Remember? I lured ye away. Ye dinnae have to be worried about yer reputation," she finished bitterly.

"*My* reputation?" he choked out. "'Tis *yer* reputation I'd be worried about, lass! If yer da kenned I'd had my tongue down yer throat when I cannae marry ye—"

When he bit off the rest of his words, she raised her head. "What? Da would do naught."

'Twas true. Everyone in the Highlands kenned Laird Oliphant was a few notes short of a folksong—which was saying rather a lot, since folksongs were, as far as she was concerned, a form of entertainment only slightly above throwing sticks into the air and betting whether they'd come down again. But aye, Da wasn't a particularly competent laird —hellfire, he wouldn't be a particularly competent *cabbage* —and her eldest sister Coira was the one who was basically running the clan these days. And neither Coira nor any of her sisters would care what Robena did with Kester MacBain.

"This isnae relevant right now, Robena," he was muttering. "What matters is that—"

"I think *'tis* relevant," she contradicted. "If my reputation matters naught, then I think ye owe me an explanation for why ye willnae even consider marriage—"

"*Someone is pinning me to the wall,*" he interrupted in a growl.

Robena's mouth snapped shut. After a moment, she whispered, "What?"

"I asked who kenned we were here," he ground out, his words falling over themselves, "because someone—or something—has pressed himself against my back. 'Tis a huge weight. I'm trying no' to crush ye."

Oh.

Well, that explained a) the delightful way he was pressed against her again and b) the fact his erection had mysteriously disappeared.

"I dinnae see anyone," she whispered. Here in the secret passages in the lower reaches of Oliphant Castle, there were enough entrances and cut-outs that light seeped in.

"I can feel him," he muttered. "And—*God's Wounds!* Something wet just slithered across my arse."

Arse.

A suspicion popped into her mind, and she squirmed about, until she could peek under one of Kester's arms.

"Bill!"

"Bill?" he groaned.

She wiggled further, until she was out from between Kester and the wall and was able to push on the gray hide happily leaning against the laird.

"Bill the ass," she clarified. "Go on, Bill!" Swatting at the dumb animal's withers was a poor substitute for smacking Kester, but it needed to be done. "Find someplace else to rest."

Kester's arms were braced against the wall, his head hanging low. "Let me get this straight. First, I broke ye, then an ass decided *I* was the ideal person to lick?"

One more swat and the stubborn animal heaved upright. "Takes one to ken one," Robena muttered.

"*Why* is there a *donkey* wandering through the secret passages of yer castle?" he snapped, pushing himself upright as Bill trotted away.

"This is his home. Surely ye noticed all the donkey shite on the floor?"

"I thought it strange enough ye had a donkey wandering through yer great hall—"

"Och, I do as well, but my mother's as strange as Da. Ye think *I* like the idea—"

He didn't let her finish. "But ye allow yer ass in the secret passages?"

She scowled up at him as she planted her fists on her hips. "He's no' *my* ass! *My* ass is the one I brought into the secret passageways myself and am now listening to yell at me about something which isnae my fault!"

She saw the exact moment he understood the insult,

because with a growl, he lunged forward and scooped up one of her hands.

Muttering something about the saints and arses and asses, Kester tugged her toward the closest entrance.

And Robena hated the fact she still loved the way her hand fit so well in his.

HER ASS!

That's what she'd called him! An ass!

Her ass.

At least she'd called him *hers*. But still…an ass?

Better than an arse.

How, exactly, was an ass better than an arse?

One's a beast of burden, one's a bifurcated bit of fat and muscle —with two dimples—ye shite out of.

Aye, he kenned the *difference* between an arse and an ass, but—

Wait, two dimples? To shite out of?

Ye've never noticed arse dimples afore? They're just above the buttocks—

Why in all the levels of hell was he having this argument with himself? *Now?*

Because 'twas easier than focusing on the hurt he saw in the eyes of the woman behind him.

When Robena stumbled coming through the exit to the secret passages—although here on the main level, with so many doors leading to the great hall that a *fooking donkey* could wander through, they were hardly *secret*—he made himself slow.

Made himself *breathe*.

God's Blood, but kissing her had been—had been…!

He didn't even have words for it.

'Twas the most magnificent experience of his life.

Aye. That.

Kester forced himself to breathe deeply, to turn to her, to exhale without cursing himself. "Milady," he said stiffly, offering her his arm.

Not that 'twould help; with the hustle and bustle in the great hall, more than a few people had seen them emerge from the wall looking disheveled. She was the laird's daughter and looked as if she'd been trysting with a rogue.

Ye're the rogue in that scenario.

Aye, he knew it.

When she placed her hand on his forearm, her fingers barely caressed his skin and he saw her swallow. She was holding herself back and he hated it.

Hated he'd done that to her.

The last weeks…one of the reasons he'd fallen so hard for this woman was her enthusiasm for life. She was an auburn-haired spitfire, constantly in motion, ready to take on the world. He'd loved listening to her goals and plans, and knew she was determined enough to see them through.

And no matter how many times he reminded himself he wouldn't—*couldn't* be here to see her succeed, he'd still found himself falling in love with her.

Ye dumb fooker.

And now he'd finally had to tell her that.

After he kissed her.

Why in damnation couldn't he have had the ballocks to tell her that *before*?

Because ye wanted to kiss her.

So, so badly. He'd wanted to kiss her *so* badly.

"My father is waving us over." Her tone was as rigid as her body language.

Glad for the excuse to look at anyone else, Kester searched

the hall until he saw the laird in front of the hearth. The old man was, in fact, waving his hand over his head.

"Is that what he's doing?" he muttered. "He looks as if he's enthusiastically waving away a fart."

Good God, did he just say that out loud? He was definitely rattled.

"Nay, Da's hand is too high for that." Robena's tone was light, as if she was one of his men, joking about such a topic. "Unless he's farting out of his mouth, which is sometimes called *belching*."

He'd hurt her. He'd *seen* the hurt in her normally laughing brown eyes. He'd felt it in the way she'd held herself—was feeling it now. All that, and she could still make him smile?

God help him, he was doomed.

He was in love with a woman he couldn't have.

By the time the pair of them wove their way through the gathered servants to stand before the Oliphant, Kester realized his man Mook stood beside the older man. He was looking somber, which meant someone had told him to be somber, because the big idiot was more than a few bricks shy of a wall.

"My lord," Kester greeted Robena's father formally. "The preparations for Lady Wynda's wedding are in place?"

"Place, aye," the older man repeated, as was his wont. He was smiling sort of vaguely as he glanced around the hall. "Coming together well, I think, although I've been told a man at a wedding is as useless as a third leg on a walnut."

Kester politely joined him in the laughter, having become used to the man's nonsensical metaphors.

"I cannae imagine why a walnut needs a third leg," spoke up Robena.

He leaned closer. "'Tis the point," he muttered from the corner of his mouth, and heard her swallow her snort of laughter.

Well, he could still make her laugh. That was good,

wasn't it?

The rumble which preceded one of Mook's statements started, and they all looked at him expectantly. After a while, he said, "My third leg has two nuts."

Kester blanched.

Laird Oliphant blinked.

And Lady Robena burst into laughter. "Och, well done, Mook! Ye're right! Two walnuts!"

"Bigger, milady," the giant rumbled.

Holy fook, did the idiot really just make a joke about the size of his ballocks to a *lady?*

Well, ye're the one who made a joke about passing gas to that same lady.

The lady in question had dropped her hold on Kester's arm in order to wrap her arm across her stomach; that's how hard she was laughing.

So, 'twas difficult to claim Mook—who was grinning hugely—had offended her.

"Do ye need some duties?" Kester snapped, wondering if Doughall—the Oliphant commander—was sparring this morning. Mook could use some sense knocked into him.

"Nay, milord," the big man drawled. "I did my dooty this morning, just like every morning."

As Robena bent double, her laughter now muffled snorts, the Oliphant grinned hugely.

"Morning, aye. We'll miss ye, hmm?"

What?

But whatever he'd said made Mook straighten. One hand—the size of a small sheep—extended, holding a scroll. "Sorry, milord, I forgot."

"Ye forgot," Kester repeated, reaching for it. "Ye forgot ye did a doo—" Nay, he wasn't going to repeat that, not with Robena still snickering.

"I forgot Pudge told me to find ye and deliver this ASAP."

Pausing in the process of unrolling it, Kester glanced at his man. "Asap? What does that mean?"

The big man shrugged. "He said that's what the King's messenger had said. Asap. He said it had to do with snakes."

"Only if ye're dyslexic," gasped Robena, obviously still recovering from her laughing fit. "I think ye mean *asps.*"

"Asps, aye," repeated her father. "Verra dangerous. One of them kicked in the head of my brother."

"Ye dinnae have a brother, Da," Robena reminded him.

"No' anymore," intoned Mook, showing surprising grasp of the situation.

Mayhap attempting to delay the inevitable—Kester's heart had begun to pound at the words *King's messenger*—he cocked his head at the banter. "Asap sounds like a singular something. What's a sap?"

"Sap, aye," repeated the older laird. "'Tis stuff that comes from trees."

"Lose yer energy," Mook threw in.

Robena was shaking her head. "Its archaic meaning is to tunnel under a fortified position. Undermine, more or less. Why are ye all looking at me like that? I share a chamber with *Wynda*, of course I ken weird words."

He had to clear his throat. "We're just wondering, lass, what *archaic* means."

"Och, 'tis easy. It means…ye ken." She gestured about. "*Now*. The dark ages."

As one, they all turned to the window.

"Doesnae look too dark to me," Mook rumbled. "Now, what's dyslexic mean?"

"Mean, aye," Robena's father repeated happily. "Forget the language lesson, what does the King say, mmm?"

Shite. Well, no use putting it off any longer.

Kester took a deep breath and unrolled the scroll in one fluid movement. Aye, there was the seal he'd expected, although 'twas likely stamped by some counselor's hand. Still, 'twas the King who ordered him to collect the missive Gordon —the royal messenger who'd died last month when he'd attempted to rape one of Robena's sisters—had left undelivered.

*THE RECIPIENTS CAN BE FOUND **at this year's Games. Your men will likely be pleased to represent the noble name of MacBain in contest against the other Highland clans.***

THE KING WAS CORRECT; Kester's men *would* look forward to the chance to test their skill against others at the yearly Highland Games. They hadn't the coin to attend last year, but they'd been on their way there this summer when they'd stopped on Oliphant land…and been delayed by a pretty set of brown eyes.

And Gordon's murder.

True.

"Well?" rumbled Mook. "Was Pudge right? Are we off to slaughter some Murray pigs?"

Kester's eyes had fallen on the last sentence. The *decree.*

His fate was sealed.

He swallowed. "Nay," he said hoarsely. "We're going to the Highland Games."

His bloody hands wanted to shake as he rolled up the parchment, so he ceased trying, and focused on breathing, instead.

Beside him, Robena had sucked in her own breath of surprise as Mook let out a whoop.

"The Games? Kester—I mean, *milord.* Ye're going to the Highland Games."

He couldn't look at her. Not after what they'd shared. Not

after what he'd read.

Instead, he held her father's gaze. "We'll stay for Lady Wynda's celebration tonight, milord, and leave tomorrow morning."

The old man nodded. "Morning, aye. The Oliphants have a long history of kicking arse—well, prodding buttock—at the Games. Mayhap I'll send a few warriors with ye to show ye how 'tis done."

Kester did his best to look pleased. "They will be welcome, milord," he managed to choke out, although his attention was fully on the woman at his side, who'd latched on to Kester's forearm. He had to fight to keep his expression impassive as the familiar heat flowed across his skin, starting where Robena touched him.

"*Kester*. The Games are almost over. By the time ye get there—"

"We'll be there in enough time," he snapped, still unable to look at her. "I've been tasked with delivering Gordon's missive." And one other mission.

One he dreaded more than any other.

Mayhap she understood. Mayhap she was just tired of him ignoring her.

Either way, Robena snatched the King's scroll from his unresisting hand.

The cowardly part of him wanted to reach for it, to tear it into pieces, to cast it into the fire before she could read the King's orders.

But he was just delaying the inevitable. The King's decision had been passed down a year ago and Kester had delayed long enough. He didn't want the alliance, but that bastard Ian Murray did, and now the King was making it official.

Now, 'tis an order.

Robena's hands were shaking when she finally looked up from the scroll. She didn't speak to her father, nor to Mook.

She just met Kester's eyes, her own shining with unshed tears.

Instinctively, he reached for her, only to remind himself *he* was the cause of her pain. His fingers curled into fists to stop himself from touching her.

"Kester," she whispered.

And he told himself he absolutely, irrevocably, beyond a shadow of a doubt, deserved this guilt. He'd done this to her. He'd fallen in love with her. He'd kissed her.

All the while knowing they had no future.

She said naught else but turned and fled.

Kester watched her go, trying to harden his heart against the pain in her eyes, telling himself it had to happen now, rather than later.

If ye'd been stronger, 'twould no' have happened at all.

Aye, but he hadn't been able to resist one last taste of pleasure before a lifetime of sorrow.

The King's message hit the floor and unrolled just slightly, so the last line, the signature, and the seal showed.

But he kept his eyes on Robena as she lifted the skirts of that beautiful yellow gown and hurried up the stairs toward the woman's solar, because he didn't *need* to read the words.

They'd been burned into his mind, his heart.

You will have another reason to celebrate. We have word the Murrays are at the Games as well. Your bride awaits. Further delay is not wise, MacBain. It is time to marry Lady Elspeth Murray, end this feud, and secure the wellbeing of your people. This marriage will bring your clan the peace and prosperity you are so anxious for.

Fook.

CHAPTER 2

THERE WAS one thing sacred in Robena's life, and that was her music. Oh, there was the *sacred* sacred stuff, like religion and the Infinite Mystery, or whatever Father John was always going on about. But music…music was….

Well, she couldn't touch it or taste it, but 'twas *there*. It always had been and always would be there for her, even when her heart felt broken and there was a hollow pit in her stomach.

Which is why, when she stomped back into the ladies' solar, she didn't throw her pipes into the corner with all the anger she felt.

Instead, she arranged them very carefully beside her lute and exhaled, trying to push aside some of the pain.

It didn't work.

Well, one of the benefits of piping was that 'twas difficult to cry while doing so. 'Twas *possible*, but between the tears and the snot and all the blowing, one tended to sound like a dying duck. So up there, on the battlements, just her and the wind and the pipes, Robena had swallowed down her tears and focused on her music.

"Are ye feeling better?"

The quiet question had Robena whirling, embarrassed that she hadn't noticed Nicola at her worktable. Her sister was calmly, delicately, mixing a draught of some sort, her expression soft as she met Robena's gaze. There was no pity in her eyes, just concern.

She was, after all, the healer.

Robena sighed, her fingertips lingering on the pipes. "Aye, a bit." She *did* feel better.

Music always helped.

Mayhap she *could* feel and taste music, in some sense.

"I'm glad," her sister said softly. "I saw yer face when ye brushed past me earlier, and I kenned ye were either on yer way to the battlements with yer pipes, or ye were going to have a good cry. Mayhap both."

She'd *tried* both. 'Twas easier to be angry than sad. "I figured there was enough commotion in the great hall that nae one would hear me."

Nicola snorted softly, her attention on the flagon into which she was sprinkling something dried and green. "We can hear ye. Ye ken they've started calling ye the Ghostly Piper of Oliphant Castle?"

"'Tis foolish." Robena threw herself down onto her stool beside her harp. "I only go up to the highest point so I willnae disturb ye down here."

"And we appreciate it." Her sister's lips curled slightly. "Harp and lute and wind instruments are one thing, but ye are particularly *enthusiastic* about the pipes."

As her fingers strummed the harp's strings, Robena felt more of the tension leave her shoulders. "I dinnae think I'm louder than other pipers."

Nicola shrugged. "I've only heard a few besides ye. I imagine, at the grand competitions or on the battlefield, a piper's music would need to be heard across a large field. So, loud is good."

"Aye," Robena mumbled in distraction, her fingers already plucking out a melody as she thought about her sister's words. "Good."

Grand competition.

The Highland Piping Competition was to be held at the end of the Highland Games.

Often the Games began with the musical competitions, but since the pipers spent the duration of the Games showing off their skills and encouraging their clan's competitors—or scaring the shite out of their opposition—the piping contest was only a formality.

For the last few years, as Robena's skill had improved, she'd learned everything she could about the Highland Piping Competition. There was a sort of perverse obsession with it, really; whereas 'twas perfectly acceptable for a lady to play the harp or lute, the pipes were a man's instrument.

And, she imagined, almost as fun as the *other* man's instrument.

Although I dinnae think ye blow into *that one.*

Whereas usually such a bad joke would make her smile— even if no one else had heard it—today she wasn't in the mood. To think that only a few hours ago she'd thought she had a chance to play with Kester's instrument!

And no' his musical instrument.

Although mayhap he'd sing if she put his—what had Wynda called it? Och, aye, his cock!—*cock* in her mouth.

Stop it.

Aye, being aroused and depressed at the same time shouldn't be possible.

"So, do ye want to talk about it?" Nicola prodded gently.

"'Tis a rather damp sensation," Robena mumbled.

"What?"

Robena's head jerked up. "*What?*"

Her sister raised a brow. "I asked if ye wanted to talk about it."

Feeling a flush working its way up her neck, Robena bent back over the harp. "Talk about what?" She tried to sound nonchalant.

And knew it didn't work when her older sister tsked.

"Talk about whatever had ye looking so upset earlier? Is it...." She hesitated. "I heard the MacBains will be moving on tomorrow."

"Aye." Robena shrugged, as if it didn't matter. "Laird MacBain received instructions from the King. They're heading to the Highland Games."

It is time you marry Lady Elspeth Murray and end this feud.

Kester was betrothed.

He'd *been* betrothed all this time. *That* was what the "further delay" part of the letter had referenced. Most of the Highlands knew the MacBains were feuding with the Murrays, and apparently the King had demanded a marriage alliance in order to end the fighting.

Kester MacBain was betrothed to the Murray's daughter, and he'd *still kissed her.*

To be fair, ye didnae really give him any choice, what with the way ye threw yerself at him. Mayhap 'tis why he resisted so long; and he did *say he couldnae marry ye.*

Great.

Now her subconscious was ganging up with her libido.

With a sigh, she dropped her forehead against her harp.

"I'll take that as a nay, ye dinnae want to talk about it," Nicola said drily. "Although I'll assume whatever has ye so upset is why ye're now calling Laird MacBain—whom ye've been calling Kester for weeks and sighing happily over—by his title."

"I have no," mumbled Robena, her left index finger plucking the same note over and over.

"Aye, ye have!" Her sister sounded ungodly cheerful, among the clink of her potions. "No' just sighing, but humming too."

"I'm a musician."

"And I found the parchment where ye wrote *Lady Robena MacBain* over and over again with flowers and hearts around it. Although why someone would want to draw a bodily organ is beyond me."

Shite.

Groaning, Robena began to knock her head against the wooden frame of her harp.

Older sisters were the absolute worst, weren't they?

Nicola was silent long enough that Robena peeked up, wondering if she'd finally been left alone. But her sister was just focused on her measuring and mixing.

After a long while, the healer said, "Kester's leaving for the Highland Games, eh?"

"*Laird MacBain* has made it verra clear his future includes a trip away from Oliphant land. Without me. His future doesnae involve me."

"He. Is going. To the. *Highland Games.*"

Robena frowned and straightened. "*Aye. He is.*" She raised a brow. "Why. Are we. Talking. *Like this?*"

Without looking up, Nicola's lips curled. "I'm trying. To make. *A point.* About the Highland Games."

Raising her hands, Robena pushed herself to her feet. "For the fourth—fifth?—time: he's going to the Highland Games!" She allowed her palms to slap down against her thighs for emphasis. "What does it matter?" Before her sister could answer, she shook her head. "I dinnae want to talk about it."

Kester was going to the Highland Games, aye. *To marry someone else.*

She felt like a complete and utter fool.

Of course, he didn't want to marry her. *Of course,* he would prefer to marry the woman who could assure peace for his clan.

He was kind and noble and worried about his people; she knew he'd do anything necessary to ensure his clan's prosperity. Even marry his enemy's daughter.

She's likely tall and beautiful and kens how to embroider.

His betrothed didn't play the pipes.

Robena could feel the tears pricking at the backs of her eyes and hated them. 'Twas better to stay angry at him—at all men!—than be hurt at his inevitable choice.

But St. Kelsi's vocal cords! The man could kiss!

She forced a scowl, forced down the memory of his touch, and stomped across the room to her sister's worktable.

"Is there aught here which will make me forget I've been a fool?" She peered over the scales and cutting boards and mysterious and herbally looking bags. "Or mayhap make everyone *else* forget I've been a fool?"

Without looking up, Nicola said mildly, "If ye're asking me to poison the entire keep during Wynda's wedding celebration tonight…the answer's nay."

"But I liked how ye paused there afore answering."

Nicola smirked. "I didnae. 'Twas me inhaling."

"Ye were *considering* it," Robena needled, leaning her weight on her forearms. "I like that."

"I'm no' poisoning people."

Robena nodded to the flagon. "What's that? It looks poisonous."

"'Tis, in too great a quantity. Anything's poisonous in too great a quantity."

"Water's no'."

Nicola finally met her eyes. "It is if ye're drowning." Her gaze sparkled with merriment.

"Hmm. How about air? Everyone needs air to live. Ye cannae have too much of it."

"Can ye fly?"

Robena's brows drew in. "Nay."

"Well, then, if ye fall off a cliff, or the highest battlement while practicing yer piping…I imagine ye'd have just enough time on the way down to decide there *is* such a thing as too much air."

Oh, by St. Kelsi's eardrums. Robena rolled her eyes. "'Tis too much *ground* that'll give ye trouble in that scenario, Nicola. Can I assume whatever ye're concocting isnae poisonous and cannae help me to fly?"

Her sister shrugged and continued stirring. "I suppose whisky *can* be said to make people fly, but nay. 'Tis just another draught for Mother.

Ah.

Mother was…a bit egalitarian with her illnesses. In that she had all of them, all the time.

"What is it?"

Nicola pulled the thin spoon from the concoction and began to clean it off. "Whisky, honey, water, and rosemary."

"Oh, so she has restless leg syndrome again?"

"Nay. When she complains of *that*, I spice her whiskey, honey, and water with *basil*. I've found if it tastes slightly different each time, she believes me."

'Twas easier to concentrate on other's complaints rather than the fact Kester was betrothed to someone else.

Robena leaned closer to sniff at the mug. "I like the rosemary. What is she complaining of this time?"

Her expression carefully neutral, Nicola announced, "Our mother has declared she is suffering from foot scald."

Robena wrinkled her nose. "Foot scald? Like…?"

"Hoof rot, aye."

"But…I thought ye could only get hoof rot if ye were—"

Nicola interrupted with a put-upon sigh. "A goat, aye."

Hm. "So…she's demanded ye treat her hoof rot? With whisky?"

The healer was trying not to smile. "She doesnae ken 'tis mostly whisky. She believes I'm a miracle worker, and all of my draughts make her nice and sleepy, and when she wakes up, her foot scald will be cured!" Her voice dropped to a mumble. "Until next time."

"And the only difference between this and her other cures is the rosemary?"

"Och, nay!" Nicola propped her hip against the worktable and crossed her arms. "The secret to healing is no' necessarily the herbs and medicines, but the other stuff. For instance, in Mother's case, I'll tell her to take a sip from this draught once every two minutes—conveniently there's a celebration tonight, so we can time it by the choruses of the songs—for the three hours afore bed." From the way Nicola's cheeks were dimpling, she was feeling mischievous. "And she must no' engage in any nagging activity—Wynda and Fen will thank me for that—for three days, and she must sleep on her left side as much as possible. Och, aye, and she has to remember to keep her hooves out of the mud."

'Twas said with such a completely dry tone, Robena burst into chuckles.

"How long have ye been plying Mother with such 'cures'?" she asked.

To her surprise, Nicolas sighed and dropped her arms. "My whole life, it feels like," she muttered, reaching for her supplies to begin cleaning up.

Robena slowly straightened, the slump of her sister's shoulders piercing her own pain. "Nicola?"

The other woman sent a smile over her shoulder, but it looked forced. "I'm fine. 'Tis just…." She shrugged as she slid the scale into place on a shelf. "Do ye ever wonder if there's *more?* I mean…we've been here on Oliphant land our whole lives."

Robena cocked a brow. "Ye want adventures? Like Leanna?" Their younger sister had always been wild and mischievous and had gone off to marry Laird McClure at the beginning of the summer. "Ye want to see the world?"

"I want…." Nicola shook her head and shrugged again as she planted her hands on her hips, her gaze locked on the shelves of her healing implements, although clearly not seeing them. "I'm no' certain what I want. But…I ken I'm supposed to help people. I've been considering…."

When she trailed off, Robena gave her a moment, then prompted quietly, "What?"

"Ye ken of the nunnery north of here? St. Dorcas the Ever Petulant?" Nicola murmured. "They've sent for me."

Robena reared back. "Ye want to be a *nun?*" She began to shake her head. "Nicola, nay! I mean, I understand wanting to be recognized, to make a difference—that's why I've always wanted to go to the Highland Piping Competition! But, to take vows? We'd never see ye again."

Unbidden, her hand rose, reaching for her sister. "Ye'd never marry, never ken a man's touch! Never hold yer babe—"

Her sister interrupted her with a harsh slash of her palm. "I'm no' *taking* vows, ye blathering dobber!" Nicola's smile was crooked and a little sad. "I'm just *visiting*. They need a healer, and I dinnae want to spend the rest of my life pouring whisky for Mother and lying about it."

Frowning thoughtfully, Robena slowly straightened and considered her sister's words. Of all of them, Nicola was the gentlest, and 'twas easy to imagine her accepting a life of quiet contemplation among the nuns. *Was* she actually considering taking vows, or had she been truthful about only visiting?

"What's this really about, Nicola?" she asked quietly.

Her sister shook her head. "Da says we have to be married. And there's nae one here I want to marry."

"That's nae reason to *join a convent!*" Robena burst out. "We've had to sit in this room and listen to Wynda go on about the joys and pleasures a man can bring a woman—remember the book?" She threw out her hand, pointing to the desk where Wynda's naughty manuscript had sat for years before being moved to her new husband's cottage. "Remember?"

"How could I forget?" Nicola asked with a wry quirk of her lips. "I'm no' giving up on finding pleasure, Robbie." She used the old nickname. "I just...ken I'm no' going to find it here."

Robena peered in suspicion. "If ye think a bunch of dusty auld nuns can help ye...."

"I'm certain quite a few of them are young and attractive," her sister announced haughtily.

Oh. "Ye...prefer the company of women?" Robena held her hands up, palms out. "Nay, nay, I'm no' judging. That's..." She cleared her throat and tried to sound enthusiastic. "I mean, *hurrah!* Mayhap a nunnery *is* exactly where ye belong."

Nicola burst into laughter.

As Robena continued to bluster about how she loved and accepted her sister for who she was, Nicola reached out and grabbed her hands, squeezing her into silence.

Still grinning, the healer held her gaze. "Thank ye for loving me. And for being concerned about me. I will be fine, and I promise ye I'll find fulfillment."

She might've meant a sort of spiritual fulfillment, except Nicola did that thing where she waggled her eyebrows mightily, and 'twas hard to take her seriously. Robena found her lips curling in response.

"So, what I want to ken...," her sister continued, "is about how *ye* are planning on being recognized. Remember what ye said earlier? Ye wanted recognition?"

"Aye." All her sisters knew Robena chafed here on Oliphant

Land where she was the best musician heard in a century. She wanted to pit herself against other pipers, wanted to know how good she really was.

Nicola lowered her chin. "The Highland Piping Competition is in a fortnight, aye? At the end of the summer? At the end of the Highland Games."

Oh, St. Kelsi's uvula, they were back to this? Robena rolled her eyes. "Aye, the *Highland Games.*"

"The Highland Games," her sister repeated. "Where...?"

"Good Lord in Heaven, ye're being cryptic!"

Nicola blew out a huff of breath, half a laugh. "The *Highland Games,* Robbie! Where Kester is going!"

Scowling, she pulled her hands from Nicola's grip. "I have decided I hate Kester MacBain, and he and his men can go toddle off to the Highland Games, and I hope a caber lands on his head!"

Her older sister was looking at her with an expression halfway between pity and laughter. As if she believed Robena was a complete idiot.

'Twas a sort of smirk.

Which, to be fair, seemed to be the basic facial expression of older sisters.

"What?" Robena snapped.

Nicola shook her head as she reached for Mother's draught. "A caber can land on his head *after* he gets ye to the Highland Games, sister. He's going, and ye might no' like him verra much, but ye—and we!—trust him to get ye there."

On her way to the door, she threw yet another smirk over her shoulder. "Da's changed his mind about sending any Oliphant warriors to the Games this year, but I'd wager the MacBain doesnae ken that. Just sort of...tag along, eh?"

And then she was gone.

And Robena exhaled.

Tag along.

Could she just…tag along?

In a thoughtful daze, she turned to her pipes.

The Highland Piping Competition was held at the end of the Highland Games. The MacBains were attending the Highland Games so Kester could marry his betrothed. His men were strong and capable, and Robena would feel safe traveling with them.…

Why couldn't she just sneak away and travel with them to the Games? She could enter the competition—oh! Mayhap as *Robbie* Oliphant! She could cut her hair—the length had always given her headaches, anyhow!—and dress as a lad, and she'd be able to compete!

Breathing heavily, she stumbled against the table, a huge grin on her face.

It could work.

It *would* work.

It all sounded rather wonderful, if one left out the phrase *"so Kester could marry his betrothed."*

Could she travel across the Highlands with him, knowing he was going to marry another woman at the end of their journey?

Well…aye. He's made his decision quite clear. He's kenned all along he couldnae be with ye because he was to marry this beautiful, talented Murray lass.

So 'twould be difficult, but the rewards were impressive. She'd be able to attend the Games *and* the Competition.

If she had her sisters tell Da that Kester was escorting her —did Da ken Kester was betrothed to someone else? If no', he'd assume the laird meant to marry *her*.

Curse her traitorous liver for giving a flip of joy at the idea.

Nay, down, liver. I'm no' marrying that arse. He kissed me, kenning full well there was nae future for us!

But…there could be a future for *her* if she was brave enough to reach out and grab it.

Almost hesitantly, her finger trailed along the pipes' bladder. Could she do it?

Tonight, after the celebrations for Wynda and Pherson's wedding died down, she could cut her hair. Nae one would look for her, especially if she had Nicola to cover for her. She could cut her hair and dress as a lad and sneak out afore dawn. She could meet up with the MacBains on their way to the Games and they'd assume she was one of the warriors her father had sent.

Well, mayhap not a *warrior*.

A finger tapped at her lips in one of Wynda's favorite gestures. She could *do this.*

A mustache might help.

A grin spilt her lips, and for the first time since she'd realized Kester was pulling away from her, her heart felt lighter with excitement.

He might have broken her future, but to hell with him! He could—mayhap without even realizing it!—help her build a *new* future!

Aye, she had a new plan. And by St. Kelsi, it *would* work.

To the Games!

CHAPTER 3

THE MACBAINS WERE AN UNUSUALLY stoic lot the morning they set off from Oliphant Castle, and it had everything to do with the amount of ale they'd consumed the night before. Pudge was the only one of the lot who looked in his usual spirits—where *usual spirits*, in his case, meant scowling—and that was only because Kester had never seen anyone who could drink as much as the grizzled veteran could and still remain upright.

Aye, his men had over-indulged the night before and were paying the price this morning. But who could blame them? The Oliphants knew how to throw a party when one of their own married…and his men had come to enjoy the hospitality of the clan.

There'd been grumbles when Kester announced they were leaving, especially when the men learned where they were headed and why. They'd miss the Oliphants.

Almost as much as Kester would.

This morning, the sun seemed too bright and their horse's steps too jarring. The land was beautiful, aye, but he doubted any of them were actually appreciating it.

For his part, Kester's sour stomach had naught to do with the ale he'd consumed at the wedding celebration they'd attended last night, and everything to do with the woman he hadn't seen.

He hadn't participated in the dancing or carousing, but spent the evening with his back to the wall, sipping at his ale, and watching for Robena. Oh, she'd attended the celebration, but hadn't danced, and had left before 'twas over.

She'd looked…disconcertedly *happy*.

Och, he *wanted* her to be happy! He wasn't disappointed by her easy smile, or the way she danced with her new brother-in-law, and held her new niece aloft. Nay, he was *glad* to see she'd moved on from the disaster in the secret passage, where he'd kissed her and then told her he couldn't marry her.

But did she have to do it so quickly?

Kester's chest felt hollow, as if he was missing something important. As if he'd left it back at Oliphant Castle….

And 'twas a little galling to realize *she'd* gotten over him so quickly.

So, aye, this was guilt and sorrow and pain all mixed together in his stomach to make him feel miserable this morning.

Mayhap he needed to eat.

"Laird, ye're certain we shouldnae have waited?" Giric was frowning as he twisted in his saddle to look over his shoulder, as if he could see the now-distant Castle. "The Oliphant said he wanted to send some warriors with us to the Games."

Before Kester could reply, Auld Gommy snorted.

"Ye're just disappointed ye couldnae stay longer," he teased the younger man. "How many lasses did ye bed last night, eh?"

Since 'twas well-known Giric was considered the handsomest man this side of Inverness, Kester wasn't surprised to see his warrior smile smugly and toss back his blond curls.

"A gentleman never reveals his conquests, Gommy. Ye'd ken that, were ye a gentleman."

"Pay nae attention to him, lad," growled Pudge. "He's just jealous he couldnae even get a lass to smile at him."

Giric shook his head. "Gommy's too auld to ken what to *do* with a lass if she smiled at him."

As Auld Gommy sputtered in anger, Weesil sidled up to Kester. "The pretty lad's right, Laird. Were we supposed to wait for Oliphant warriors?"

Kester stifled his sigh, unwilling to admit he'd been as anxious to depart the place of hard memories as his men had been to stay.

"We didnae leave until after dawn, Weesil. If he'd intended to send men along, they would've been waiting."

"After a night of carousing?" The skinny man always spoke quietly, almost too low to hear. The others claimed his voice was as devious as the rest of him, but he was a good man in a fight, and his clansmen trusted him. Mostly.

Just dinnae bet against him.

Kester shook his head. "We're still on Oliphant land. If they want to join us, they'll catch up."

From up ahead, there came a familiar rumbling. All the MacBains looked expectantly at the large figure on the larger horse who led them.

"Or they'll wait for us," Mook shouted.

Well, it wasn't a shout, but he seemed as incapable of modulating his volume as Weesil...just in the opposite direction.

"What do ye mean?" growled Pudge, kneeing his horse into a trot to catch up with Mook, who had extended a long arm toward a thicket by a bend in the path.

"Ambush, Laird?" murmured Weesil, his hands dropping to one of the dozen knives strapped to various belts.

Kester held up a hand to halt his man from pulling a blade.

With the number of them, 'twas more likely Weesil would stab himself or slice off a pertinent article of clothing.

And having seen Weesil's naked backside once—Kester shuddered, remembering that particularly strange reaving adventure last autumn—there was no need to see it again.

"Hold. We'll see what Pudge finds."

Still, Kester's hand dropped to his sword's hilt as well.

Just in case.

A man didn't spend four years fighting a slash-and-grab feud with the Murrays and *not* expect trouble, even this far onto an ally's land.

From up ahead, Pudge growled, "Who in the fook are *ye?*" at the same time Mook bellowed, "Hello, pretty lad!"

Giric's horse jumped forward. *Mayhap* the animal was just twitchy, or mayhap the warrior wanted a look at whomever Mook would call "pretty lad".

Auld Gommy had also pushed forward, but now he clucked at his horse to step out of the way, because the path had become crowded as a seventh animal stepped from the other side of the thicket.

Kester had *heard* of people describing their jaws as dropping but had never actually experienced it...until that moment.

"Well, hello lad," Gommy cackled. "Are ye lost?"

"Dinnae be stupid, auld man," Giric announced with a toss of his head. "He's wearing the Oliphant plaid, is he no'? 'Tis one of the warriors his laird is sending to the Games. He must've left afore us and has been waiting."

Mook waved a hand the size of a side of mutton. "Hello. I'm Mook."

Weesil shifted forward in his saddle. "I dinnae recognize the lad. Is he alone?"

Since the skinny man never trusted anyone, the rest of the warriors ignored him.

Pudge frowned as he peered closer at the newcomer. "Is Giric right? Yer laird sent ye to tag along with us to the Games? Ye dinnae look like a warrior."

The newcomer, with cropped auburn curls barely contained by a leather thong, was staring wide-eyed at Kester, likely expecting him to object.

Kester couldn't, of course, because he couldn't seem to make his damn voice work.

Finally, the figure shifted in the saddle—there were strange bundles strapped all over, and not a single weapon for protection, the wee dobber—and shook auburn curls at Pudge.

"Nay." The voice was unnaturally gruff, as if a pretense. "I...I am no' a warrior. I'll leave it to the lot of ye to throw shite at each other. I'm a piper."

"Och, he's attending the contests!" Gommy burst out. "That makes more sense!"

He?

"I'm hoping 'tis his instruments strapped to his saddle," Giric agreed dryly, "and no' some strange collection of dismembered body parts."

His?

Pudge clucked his tongue. "Leave it to *ye* to think of dismembered body parts. The lad's *obviously* carrying his instruments. That's a lute," he said with a nod.

The lad?

With a snicker, Gommy stroked his beard. "*Instruments.* Sounds like a metaphor."

"What's a metty for?" rumbled Mook.

"I dunno," Weesil hissed. "What *is* it for?"

"Penis!" Gommy cackled at some joke. "That lad's got an instrument metaphor for his penis!"

His penis?

"Is it food?" Mook reached for the newcomer's saddle. "Did ye bring food, lad?"

"Enough," growled Kester.

His men fell silent and turned expectant stares his way. A new set of warm brown eyes joined them, and he marshalled his defenses.

How in the hellfire were they calling this shapely beauty a *lad?*

He had to get to the bottom of this. 'Twas one thing for her to torment him in his dreams, another thing altogether to show up and torment him when he was supposed to be focused on his clan's future!

Because, aye...she might be wearing an Oliphant kilt low on her hips to disguise her curves, and aye, she might've glued some hair to her upper lip in a shite impersonation of a mustache.... But as sure as he sat there glowering, that was Robena Oliphant watching him with wide, scared eyes.

And as surprised and confused as he was, a part of him was happy to see her. *Verra* happy to see her. And determined to ease her fear.

Nay, she shouldnae have followed us.

"What in damnation are ye doing here?" he finally asked.

"My fa—Laird Oliphant said he was sending warriors, aye? Well...." A pause for a throat-clearing. "Nae warriors wanted to attend the Games this late, but the piping competition takes place at the end of the Games, and I aim to win."

Well, fook.

He'd known Robena was a talented musician. Although she'd never mentioned piping, it made sense she'd be talented in that regard as well.

A sudden suspicion had him frowning, remembering the way the castle would sometimes be beset by ghostly piping from the highest battlements.

"'Tis good to have a goal, lad." Auld Gommy was nodding approvingly. "What's yer name?"

Kester had had enough. "Roben—"

But she interrupted. "Robbie!" she blurted frantically, holding his gaze. "Robbie Oliphant."

Robbie.

A fortnight ago, he'd met her bastard brother, a man who traveled the Highlands on missions from the King. He'd called Robena "Robbie" and it seemed as if she'd decided this would be her new name.

Damnation.

"All of ye, take a piss break," he finally growled. "I'll speak with—" He couldn't bring himself to call her a *him*, not when 'twas obvious she wasn't. "I'll speak with Robbie."

Good-naturedly, the men spread out, swinging out of their saddles and pulling out food for a meal as they moved off the path.

Kester nudged his horse into motion. When he stopped beside her, both animals shied a few steps, and he saw her confidence in gaining control of her mount.

His knee brushed against hers, but she didn't seem to notice. How *couldn't* she? He noticed everything about her; from the way her knuckles were white around the reins to the twitch of her lip which told him her false mustache tickled.

'Twas the sight of that…that *thing*, which held his attention.

"What in the name of St. John the Apostle did ye *do* to yerself?"

Her chin went up mulish. "I dinnae ken what ye mean."

Irritated with himself for blurting out such a question, he scowled as he flicked his fingers toward her lips. "Did ye glue a caterpillar to yer face? Because that is what it looks like."

One set of fingertips rose to press the clump of hair farther against her skin. "'Tis a mustache," she mumbled, no longer able to meet his eyes.

"Were ye hoping to pass as a lad at the competition?" He

softened his tone, knowing 'twas anger at himself that had him irritable. "'Twill never work. Ye're far too beautiful—"

Her gaze snapped to his. "Aye, 'twill work," she interrupted. "Yer men look at me and see a lad."

"My men are obviously blind."

"'Tis the mustache," she declared smugly.

He cocked his head as he studied her. Nay, 'twas not the mustache—or rather, not *only* the mustache. 'Twas the assurance in the way she rode, the boldness in how she met his eyes. Robena's shoulders were wider, her face broader, than some of her sisters. He knew—from long walks with her through the gardens—that she didn't consider herself beautiful, but she was wrong.

Her beauty was strength and power and confidence.

Which, with a mustache, aye, helped disguise her as a lad.

She smirked at him. "I'm right, are I no'?"

"Ye're going back to Oliphant Castle, is what ye're doing."

Her horse stepped sideways, and 'twas easy to imagine it being a response to some subtle reaction of hers.

"Ye'd lose a day of travel to take me back now, and I ken ye'd no' send me alone."

She was right, of course. He was still irritated she'd come all this way without a weapon to defend herself against wild animals or wilder men. Mayhap she felt protected since she was still on Oliphant land?

"Ye think I wouldnae welcome the delay?" he growled, leaning far enough to one side to clamp a hand on her knee. "Ye think I wouldnae appreciate the chance to postpone my fate?"

Her big brown eyes had grown even wider and he didn't miss the way her pulse jumped in her throat as she stared at him.

That wasn't fear he saw…'twas desire. And beneath his kilt,

his cock jumped in response right about the same time he realized where his hand was.

Her knee.

Her *bare* knee.

The lass was wearing a kilt, which had hiked up on one side, and he was *holding* her *bare* knee. With his *hand*. Which was *on her knee*.

He likely should have some sort of response to that, but at that moment, his mind seemed stuck on those relevant thoughts: *hand knee bare cock hand bare.*

"Kester," she whispered, her lips barely moving, and he found himself leaning toward her, as she leaned toward him.

Thank the saints she caught herself, gave herself a little shake.

"Laird MacBain." She straightened in her saddle. "I ken ye *capable* of returning me to—to Oliphant Castle." Her emphasis made him wonder if she understood his feelings about the delay. "But I ask ye to reconsider."

She was being so formal and stiff.

Like yer cock.

He winced, knowing he deserved both miseries.

And then her hand dropped atop his. "Please."

She wasn't begging. She wasn't demanding. She was just... being polite, her tone unusually empty.

He knew her well enough to know she had control over her tone. So, if that's how she sounded, that's how she *wanted* to sound.

He hated it.

He hated that mustache, he hated her sitting over there on her saddle instead of being curled up in his lap where he wanted her.

He hated Ian Murray for taking the meadow and the prime planting land which should belong to the MacBains, and he hated his sense of honor which had forced him to retaliate, leading to the King's decree.

He hated that, without the meadow and its resources, his people suffered.

He hated that his future was not his own, but belonged to his clan.

He swallowed down his anger, knowing it wasn't directed at this woman.

"Robena." He lowered his voice, although he told himself 'twas not to protect this ridiculous charade. "Ye *cannae* come to the Games with us, even if 'tis only to participate in the piping contests."

"Why no'?"

"Well, for one thing, ye're a woman."

Her chin rose as she pointed at her lip. "*Mustache.*"

With her hand removed from his, he forced himself to stop touching her bare knee. 'Twas hard.

Like his—

Nay, stop thinking about yer cock, we're all tired of hearing about it.

"A lady cannae go gallivanting across the Highlands with only a band of men from a different clan." He tried to frown. "It just isnae done."

She became interested in her horse's mane. "'Tis done if *I* do it."

"Think of yer reputation, lass!" he burst out.

"Shhh!" She darted a glance over his shoulder, but his men were laughing loudly about something, clearly in better spirits now they had something in their stomachs. "No' so loud."

"They'll see through yer disguise soon enough."

She glared at him. "No' if ye keep yer mouth shut. Call me *Robbie*, and they'll follow."

"It doesnae matter, because ye're no' coming with us to the Games."

When she shifted in her saddle, her horse shied slightly. "What if I told ye I had my father's permission to be here?"

He narrowed his eyes. That *would* change his opinion. The Oliphant was absent-minded, 'twas clear, but he *had* said he wanted to send men to the Games. Was *Robena* who he'd meant?

"Do ye? Have yer da's permission?"

Her chin rose again, her gaze firmly on his chin. "My family kens how important 'tis to me to prove my talent. They ken where I am."

"Right now?"

Stiffly, she nodded.

Bah, he'd hurt her so badly she couldn't even meet his eyes now. He wondered, if she did, would he see anger in there? Or just...more emptiness? She'd seemed to *hurt* in the secret passageway, and later, when she'd read the King's decree...but was it possible she'd gotten over him so quickly?

Yer ego can take the blow, ye arse.

Aye. He sighed.

'Twould be far better if she wasn't drowning in pain, the way he was. 'Twould be far better for her to have moved on, to have accepted her future didn't lie with him.

'Twould make him happier to ken he was responsible for only his own pain, not hers as well.

"Laird MacBain, I'm going to do this," she declared intensely. "With or without yer help, I'm going to the piping competition."

He shook his head. "If this got out, yer reputation would be shattered."

"My reputation? I'm *wearing* a *mustache*."

His lips twitched reluctantly. "Fair point, well made. But...." He winced, knowing what he had to say. "Lass, what we shared...'tis over."

'Twas the wrong thing to point out, judging from how her

expression clouded. "Of course." Her brows lowered and she glanced away. "Ye have a wedding to look forward to, and a bride to satisfy."

Fook.

He wanted to marry Ian Murray's eldest daughter about as much as he wanted to embroider, which is to say, not at all. But he'd learn to stitch frilly little flowers and shite all over his cuffs, if 'tis what it took to protect his people and convince Murray to stop pestering the King for an alliance.

He stifled a sigh. "Aye."

She flinched at his curtness, and he reminded himself 'twas for the best. "The wedding will take place at the end of the Games, same as the piping competition."

Her jaw hardened. "I wish ye and yer Murray bride much happiness. May yer marriage be blessed with many bairns."

Bairns?

The traditional wedding wish knotted his stomach. He didn't want little half-Murray bairns!

But what he wanted was irrelevant. Ian Murray had the King's ear, and the man was determined to get around giving the MacBains what was theirs, so he offered terms Kester *had* to meet.

"It'll bring peace," he growled. "That is what's important."

"Och, verra important." Her tone was mocking flippant, as she pretended interest in whatever Mook was miming. "Ye'll forgive me if I dinnae attend yer nuptials? I'll have a piping competition to win."

'Twas *good* she was angry at him. Aye.

So why did he feel like a snake?

"I understand, lass."

If looks could kill, he'd be bleeding from her sharp glance. "Stop *calling* me that!"

Och, aye. She was supposed to be a lad.

And if she joined them on their journey to the Games, he'd

have to remember that. She needed to appear as a lad in order to join the competitions. If anyone discovered who she really was, her good name would be mocked from Skye to Scone.

He had to keep her—and her reputation—safe.

"Kest—*Laird MacBain*, will ye keep my secret?"

Och, lass, I'd keep all yer secrets.

If only the King would allow it.

"If yer family approves of ye tagging along with us, then aye." He exhaled and nudged his horse away from hers. "We'll get ye to the competition, and I look forward to hearing ye play. I ken 'twill be remarkable."

Her gaze jerked up to meet his, then away just as quickly.

But in that moment, he didn't see formality or emptiness... he saw longing.

Shite.

To Kester's consternation, she was right.

His men didn't see her beauty; they saw the dirt she'd rubbed on her cheeks. They didn't see her curves; they saw the way she handled a horse. They didn't see her grace; they saw the way she laughed as loud as Mook at one of Giric's rude jokes.

'Twas the bloody mustache.

She'd glued a hank of hair—hair she'd chopped off her own head—to her lip, and now his men thought she was a lad.

They were all idiots.

Kester spent the rest of the day stewing. He allowed Pudge and Mook to lead, while he trailed behind. He told himself 'twas to keep watch for danger and to ensure Robena didn't wander off the trail...but really 'twas so he could watch her.

He watched how easily she sat on the horse, how confidently her fingers brushed against her wrapped bundles every so often. He watched her laugh with Giric and tried not to feel jealous when his man slapped her on the back in companionship. He watched her speaking quietly with Auld Gommy until the old man began to chortle.

And he watched how, every few miles, she glanced over her shoulder at Kester.

He tried not to respond to that.

Tried and failed.

Each time she met his eyes his chest tightened a bit, and stayed tight long after she'd turned back around. He found himself looking forward to those glances, wondering—*hoping*—when they'd come.

Ye're a glutton for punishment.

Aye, he must be.

But…he felt *better* with her along. Even if she wasn't speaking to him, even if she was spitting fire at him with those glances, he felt better with her nearby.

The glutton for punishment thing again.

They made it a good distance that day, and then made camp with the ease of many travels together. These men had been with him for many years—since his father's passing had made him laird and dropped a load of heaping shite in his lap—and Kester trusted them implicitly.

That didn't mean he didn't want to murder Giric when the handsome man slung his arm around Robena's shoulders, or punch Pudge when the grizzled veteran made her smile about something.

How in the name of *fook* did these arseholes not see her as a woman? They'd *all* met Lady Robena Oliphant, the laird's talented daughter, more than once. But now they were willing to admit she was a lad?

'Tis the mustache. Verra convincing.

Since they weren't a'reaving, Auld Gommy set out to make a stew with the leather-wrapped pot he'd dragged along 'Twas after sundown afore he finally declared the stew simmered long enough, but they had hard bread from the Oliphant kitchens to hold them over.

'Twas well worth the wait. Even Pudge complimented the chef, which led to Weesil clutching his chest theatrically.

"God above, I must be dying! What's next, Pudge? Are ye going to smile?"

Even Robena smirked at that.

Otherwise, she sat quietly, clearly unused to the wilderness after dark. The way she sat—her arms wrapped around her knees and her shoulders hunched toward the fire—made two things very clear:

1. She wasn't comfortable with the sounds of the forest, and
2. She really had no idea how to sit in a kilt.

He tried not to stare at the intriguing shadows behind her heels, knowing if his men noticed, they'd think him ogling a lad's crotch. But 'twas difficult. The skin of her legs was smooth and creamy, obviously unused to sunlight...and he'd had his hand on her bare knee earlier.

God's Blood, no' this again.

From where he leaned against the trunk of an old oak, outside the fire's light, Kester watched her and tried to convince his cock not to respond. He wanted her, aye, but he couldn't have her. He didn't want to hurt her like that.

Not again.

He watched his men tease her like one of them, watched her demure when they demanded a song, claiming exhaustion. Watched her watching Weesil and Mook wrap themselves in their plaid and settle in comfortable patches of grass.

Watched her realize she had no idea what the hell she was doing.

Kester pushed away from his tree and strode toward where he'd left his saddle. He pulled a blanket from beneath it —'twould smell, but she wanted to be thought a lad, eh?—and turned back to the fire.

She was still standing, her arms around her waist, hesitantly watching the other men bed down for the night.

"Here," he said gruffly, thrusting the blanket toward her, then nodding toward the tree. "There's a patch of grass over there."

"My—thanks." She hesitated only a moment before snatching the blanket and ducking around him.

He waited until she'd swung the blanket around her shoulder and laid down in the grass before he headed toward her.

Flustered, she shot upright. "What are ye doing?" she hissed as he sat beside her.

"I'm getting comfortable." He jerked his chin toward the grass and pulled his plaid up around his shoulders. "Ye should as well."

"I—I cannae sleep beside ye!"

Since she'd kept her voice low, he did the same.

"*Robbie* wouldnae mind a warm back against his, would he? Especially if 'tis his first night sleeping beside a fire in the wilderness?"

When she just set her jaw mulishly, he lowered his voice further. "Besides, if ye think I'm going to allow any of these bastards to sleep beside ye, ye're mistaken."

Her gaze snapped to his. "Ye dinnae trust yer men?"

"I trust them with my life."

I just dinnae trust them with ye.

The dying embers threw out enough light for him to watch her swallow. "And ye, Laird MacBain?" she whispered. "Can I trust ye?"

Dagger. Heart. Twist.

Ugh.

Instead of answering, he made a point to turn his back to her, to hide behind his plaid. "Go to sleep, *Robbie*. We have a long journey ahead of us."

To the Games.

"To yer wedding."

'Twas said quietly enough he thought he might've imagined it. But then he felt her back settle against his, in the ancient position of two comrades watching out for one another. It should've been comfortable, but it wasn't.

Because of the hurt in her voice.

CHAPTER 4

SHE WAS WARM. *So* warm.

A smelly horse blanket shouldn't—*oh*. There was a body at her back, the *front* of a body.

'Twas Kester. He was curled around her, both of them lying on their sides, and despite the hard ground, despite the lack of a pillow, Robena didn't think she'd ever slept more comfortably.

Except….

There was a hardness pressed into her backside, one she recognized. One she wanted.

One she couldn't have.

Damn Lady Elspeth Murray and her beauty!

Robena squeezed her eyes shut and tried not to feel comforted by Kester's arm around her middle.

She vowed then and there to write a biting, witty song disparaging his soon-to-be-bride.

There once was a lass from Clan Murray,
Whose chin was surprisingly furry.
She snorted when she laughed,
And refused to take a bath,

And her actions caused her father to wor—

Mayhap she should reconsider casting dispersions on the other lass's reputation. Especially since she was lying here in the predawn darkness with said lass's betrothed.

Trying not to enjoy it.

Desperately failing.

St. Kelsi, help me to be strong.

He'd made his choice. She wouldn't humble herself.

Unbidden, her hips flexed backwards so her rear end could cradle his hardness.

Are ye no' listening? Ye said ye wouldnae humble yerself!

Aye, but mayhap a *little* fondling....

She felt the moment he awoke. One second, Kester was soft and cozy against her back—except for one part of him which very much was the opposite of soft—and the next, he'd stiffened and rolled away from her.

As if she were a leper. Or on fire. Or a leper who was on fire.

Ye're getting strangely morbid.

Well, who could blame her? She'd had a rough few days.

She saved her sigh until she felt him push himself to his feet and stomp away, and then she wrapped her arms around herself to try to mimic his warmth.

It didn't work.

The MacBain men were an interesting lot. Her eldest sister, Coira, had interacted plenty with the Oliphant warriors...but Pudge was the only one Robena had spent any time with over the last month, and even that was limited to sitting beside him at a few meals, listening to him praise his laird. 'Twas from Pudge that Robena had learned of Kester's unfailing devotion to his clan, and how he'd put his own life on the line many times to protect his men.

So *of course*, he'd sign right up for marrying his enemy's daughter if it meant ensuring his clan's future.

But other than Pudge's praise, she only knew the rest of the MacBains by sight.

As the day progressed, she got to know them each better.

Auld Gommy was the band's cook—because he was "auld enough to ken how to make something from practically nothing," according to Giric—although Gommy assured her he was still "nimble and agile with a sword, lad, and I dinnae mean a blade!" She'd laughed along with the others, despite feeling that mayhap she should be nauseated by such a claim. His legs —where they stuck out from his kilt—were like kindling sticks, and his beard was long enough to wrap around his neck for warmth...but he was quick to offer well-meaning advice.

Even if few of them asked.

Pudge was the grumpy one, who always seemed to have a skin of *something* strong-smelling at hand. He wasn't as old as Gommy and his face was more *weathered* and less wrinkled... where the *weathered* wasn't sunshine and rainbows, but rather thunderstorms and lightning bolts. Secretly, she called him Craggy.

Because his expression was just one giant *crag*.

He and Mook rode point together throughout the day because they both were at peace with their own thoughts, and didn't need to blather, as Wynda called it. Pudge, because he didn't seem to want anything to do with other humans, and Mook because....

Well, if Pudge was a crag, then Mook was a mountain: huge, hard, and with a head full of rocks.

But he liked to laugh—even if 'twas at things like frogs and leaves and Giric's cock jokes—and Robena couldn't help but like him.

Giric was likeable as well, although his handsome face made her uncomfortable at the beginning. She could tell he was used to being able to charm others, and she tried extra hard not to give herself away.

But right around the time he complimented her on her mustache and lowered his voice to ask for tips on how she got it so thick and luxurious, Robena realized she had nothing to fear.

Weesil, on the other hand, had a way of watching her suspiciously that made her want to hunch over her saddle and hope he looked away. But by the afternoon of the second day, she realized he looked at *everyone* and everything that way… and she discovered why he was so interested in her. Or more importantly, her lute.

"Ye're a bard, aye? Do ye make up songs?" He had black, oily hair, and dark eyes that flashed with interest as he sidled up to her. He was fondling the hilt of one dagger. "Have ye made up songs about battles?"

She thought fast. "Och, aye, of course. Plenty. Dozens. Loads." *Zero, but how hard can it be?* "Blood and heads being hacked off and entrails and whatnot."

"Whatnot," snorted Auld Gommy on her other side. "Ye stick with us, lad, and we'll show ye what ye *really* need to ken to write a good song!"

And *that* is how Lady Robena Oliphant spent four hours astride a horse listening to detailed accounts of…well, blood and heads being hacked off and entrails and whatnot. The MacBain warriors were intent on ensuring she understood how to properly craft a battle ballad.

Every once in a while, she'd turn in her saddle just far enough to see Kester. Most of the time he was watching her, his expression impassive, and she looked away before so long a time passed that he'd be expected to respond to her.

But she could feel the heat of his gaze on her.

And tried not to feel comforted.

That evening, they purchased food from a crofter and

made camp beside a stream. 'Twas peaceful, but Robena could barely hold her eyes open. Two days in the saddle was more than she ever considered herself capable of, and she had many more days to go.

But 'twould be worth it, to stand in front of the best pipers in the Highlands and try her skills against them. At least, that's what she told herself as she wrapped her exhausted body in a borrowed blanket and curled up right outside of the circle of firelight.

And when she felt Kester stretch out beside her, it seemed natural to roll toward his warmth and inhale his scent and imagine things were different.

THE NEXT DAYS WERE SIMILAR, and the fun band of MacBains made their way across the Highlands. Her thighs and lower back were battered into jelly, then slowly grew tough enough that she no longer had to bite back her groans when she dismounted.

Then men accepted her as one of their own, although they teased her mercilessly about always disappearing behind a bush to do her business, when the rest of them saw no harm in lifting their kilts out of the way and pissing right beside the road.

And Kester.... Well, at night, he continued to lay down beside her, offering her his heat and protection, but during the day he held himself apart.

At Oliphant Castle, she didn't recall him separating himself from his men, and he certainly wasn't the kind of laird who considered himself better than everyone else, so she had to assume the variable here was *her*. He was holding himself separate because *she* was part of his troop now.

That is fine. That's what ye want.

Aye, 'twas…and then again, nay.

She *missed* him, which was stupid. Only a sennight ago, they were walking together in the gardens, laughing beside one another at meals. Then, those kisses…and he told her the truth; told her he couldn't be with her because he was betrothed to Lady Elspeth Murray. She'd been heartbroken, but the very next day embarked on this mad scheme.

She hadn't given herself time to mourn him, and now she was with him every day…except she also wasn't.

And thinking on it too long will give ye a headache. He made his preferences kenned, and ye have yer music to focus on.

The men were surprisingly supportive of her music. Sometimes, during the ride, Mook would ask her to play her lute. She'd mastered the art of guiding the horse without the use of her hands so she could play for them.

And all of them—even Pudge—offered her praise and appreciation when she played. Sometimes she even sang, pitching her voice as low as she dared without hurting herself in order to sound more like a lad.

After her songs, Weesil would inevitably offer her suggestions for lyrics, and Auld Gommy would holler something crude, and they'd try to yell over one another in their advice on how to improve the songs.

Often, it involved rhymes for "behead" or "eviscerate." She was coming to learn the MacBains were a cheerfully blood-thirsty lot.

"Anyhow, thank the saints I slid off the horse's back at that moment, or I'd be missing more of my ear!" Auld Gommy was saying as he leaned sideways in the saddle and lifted part of his beard—or mayhap 'twas his hair-it all seemed to flow together—to show her the long-healed scar where his lobe used to be.

From ahead of them, Pudge called back, "Why the fook were ye no' in a saddle, auld man?"

"They hadnae been invented yet!" quipped Giric before Gommy could respond. "I'm surprised they had *horses.*"

"Och, well, I *said* horse," agreed Auld Gommy good-naturedly, "but 'twas afore their domestication, truthfully. We had to go to war on trained mountain goats."

"Goats?" rumbled Mook.

"Aye, laddie, took us a fortnight to catch and fit them with their special goat-sized war helmets, if we worked day and night."

"How'd ye work through the night afore the invention of fire?" scoffed Weesil. "By the light of the moon?"

"Nay!" hooted Giric, "He used his own earwax to make candles!"

Auld Gommy pretended disappointment. "I've told ye this story already, have I?"

And Robena had to remember to keep her laugh as masculine as possible, which was difficult.

Aye, the MacBain men seemed to enjoy having a new set of ears around to listen to their stories of bravery and might—most of which she suspected were made up in an attempt to out-do one another.

But those stories were preferable to the ones about…well, sex.

Now, Robena was no prude. She was a virgin, aye, but not innocent. For years, her sister Wynda—with whom she shared a chamber—had been working on a manuscript of coital positions. She'd finally finished it, right before her marriage to Pherson, but her sisters had spent many years looking over her shoulder and learning new and interesting things about bodies. Their own *and* men's.

Hellfire, Robena had even modeled for some of the illustrations!

But even with that knowledge, the MacBain men were…a bit much. 'Twas one thing to read a description of *The Clinging*

Vine…and quite another thing altogether to see Weesil enthusiastically acting it out, complete with grunts and squeals.

"—she took it on her face!"

As the rest of the men roared with laughter, Robena kept her own face averted, knowing 'twas bright red, and knowing the men would tease her as an untried lad if they saw.

Mook sighed happily. "That's my favorite part."

"What, ye big lug?" growled Pudge.

The large warrior made a crude pumping gesture with his fist near his lap, and then opened his hand, as if releasing something. "*Aaaaah.* That part."

"Och, aye, 'tis my favorite part as well," sighed Giric.

"'Tis the *only* part!" snapped Pudge. "There's nae other part to fooking, is there?"

Giric scoffed. "There's the lead-up. Ye ken, the tits, and the bit where she fondles yer willie."

St. Kelsi save us from idiots. Did these men really think the orgasm was the *only* part of making love?

"Well, the fondling is nice," Giric allowed. "But the *aaaaahhh* is the favorite part."

"Seems Robbie doesnae think so. Ye've got the lad blushing like an apple!" Weesil snickered.

Robena lifted a hand to her mouth and was—as always—surprised when her fingers encountered the mustache. It had become a part of her, one she barely noticed anymore, even while eating…although those first few days had been difficult. Now, each morning, she touched up the glue with a small pot she'd brought along and tried not to think of it.

'Twas after all, the heart of her disguise.

"Ye dinnae think 'tis the best part of sex?" Giric demanded, pinning her with a disbelieving stare. "The *aaah.*" He made the jerking gesture again. "Spilling yer seed?"

St. Kelsi help me. Help us all.

"I think…" she hesitantly began. "I think 'tis a *good* part, aye. But the intimacy, the touching—"

"He thinks *cuddling's* the best part of sex!" hooted Giric, throwing a punch at Mook's arm which didn't rock the big man, but caused their horses to shy.

The other men chuckled, except for Auld Gommy, who came to her rescue. "Lads, when ye get as auld as I am, ye realize there's some benefit to no' always going at a lass like a randy buck. Some finesse, aye, and cuddling, willnae be amiss."

"He's just saying that because his cock needs a chance to recover!" Pudge growled, and the rest hooted with laughter.

In an effort to avoid looking at Gommy—St. Kelsi's eardrum, could her cheeks get any warmer?—Robena turned in the saddle to glance back at Kester.

As he'd been for the last few days, the man she'd thought she loved sat tall in the saddle, one hand resting loosely on the hilt of his sword as he kept watch over them all. Except...now, he was looking at her.

This wasn't any different than the hundreds of times she'd glanced back at him over the last days, but *those* times weren't in the midst of discussing cocks.

Slowly, Kester raised one brow.

And aye, it turned out her cheeks *could* get warmer. She felt her whole *body* flush in response to that little acknowledgement, and twisted back into position so quickly she felt her blood swirl in her temples.

Unfortunately, the men had noticed her distraction, and changed their stories from fables of their own prowess to those about their laird.

Robena kept her chin tucked against her chest.

'Twas one thing to hear stories of Kester's success with the ladies, or how impressive his manhood was...and another thing to remember the way that hardness had felt pressed against her, and how it had left her wet and needing.

Now is no' the time.

"One time I was hanging over the edge of a cliff," Auld Gommy was saying, "and ye ken how the MacBain will do aught to save a clansman? Well he didnae have a rope with him, so he threw me the only thing he had!"

Robena groaned and lowered her forehead to her horse's neck.

"'Tis that long?" laughed Giric.

Gommy continued, "Aye, he threw me his wee willie and saved my life!"

From up ahead, Mook rumbled, "I had a cousin named Wee Willie."

"Nay, lad, he's Wee Wullie," Pudge corrected with a sigh. "Gommy's talking of the laird's cock."

"The MacBain brought a chicken?" Mook asked, twisting in his saddle.

Since Robena's eyes were closed, she had no warning when Weesil leaned over and socked her shoulder, which she was coming to realize was a prime method of communication with these men.

Rubbing her shoulder, she sat up. "What was that for?"

"I'll wager ye could write a song about our laird's member, eh? An ode to his manhood?"

St. Kelsi, nay.

But to appease them—and to shut them up—she reached for her lute and began to strum, frantically thinking of rhymes.

"Wee Willie Winkie,

Running through the town.

Up the streets and down the streets,

In his nightgown."

Mook leaned sideways. "What's a nightgown?" he whispered over-loud to Pudge, who shook his head.

"Likely a metaphor for something," he growled. "Who ever heard of a cock running about?"

"Sounds cold," quipped Weesil.

Giric was grinning, of course. "This is the first recorded use of the word nightgown in human history!"

"Recorded?" murmured Robena.

The handsome man waved airily. "Quick! Someone write it down!"

Thank the saints the conversation devolved into an argument about what to wear at night, and whether it mattered if one was alone in the bed.

Robena did her best to ignore said conversation and strummed lightly on her lute's strings.

The high spirits lasted through that evening when they stopped to make camp in a clearing not far from the road. As Auld Gommy began to cook, a few of the men disappeared into the trees.

"There's a small loch a ways in that direction," the ancient Scot explained, throwing his beard over his shoulder as he stirred. "And bathing sounds nice after so many days in the saddle."

She hummed in agreement, wondering if she could sneak away after dark to make use of the water herself. "'Tis likely freezing."

"No' as bad as smelling like a horse for the rest of the journey," growled Pudge, who settled beside her, his back to the same fallen log. "Take some friendly advice, Robbie lad, and go wash yer bits, eh?"

Robena did *not* sniff her own armpits, but 'twas a struggle.

"Can I ask a question?" She exhaled as she rested her head against the log, the tension of sitting in the saddle all day draining away. "*Why* are ye MacBains such a battlesome lot? Who are ye fighting all the time, in these stories?"

Weesil was sitting cross-legged on the other side of the fire, dragging a whetstone along his blades, and looked up in surprise. "Och, the Murrays, of course."

"The *hated* Murrays," Pudge corrected, and Weesil nodded in agreement.

It is time to marry Lady Elspeth Murray and end this feud.

"Ye're feuding with the Murrays, aye?"

Auld Gommy snorted as he settled himself in front of a stump, where he began to mix oats and water to make bannocks. "'Tis nae our choice. I'm auld enough to remember when we considered them friends. We fought the Sutherlands then, and the Clynes, but that was just because 'twas traditional."

"What happened?" Robena asked quietly. "If ye used to be friends with the Murrays?"

"Laird Ian Murray happened, lad," barked Pudge. "And Kester's Meadow."

Her head snapped up. "Kester's Meadow?"

Weesil took up the story, his hands never stopping. "Our laird's mother was Abigail Kester, a bonny lass with bonnier blue eyes. She was a cousin to Ian Murray, who had been newly made laird of his clan. 'Twas a sort of alliance, to marry Lady Abigail to Kester's da, the auld laird. As part of the bargain, Murray included a fertile meadow which stands between our lands."

"Lady Abigail lasted long enough to birth Kester," Auld Gommy continued somberly, "and name the lad after her people."

"She died?" Robena whispered.

"Aye," grunted Pudge. "And our laird mourned her fiercely, but with a wee bairn, the clan had a focus. 'Twas a year later that Murray announced he was taking back the meadow he'd given us as part of the marriage contract."

Auld Gommy nodded as he mixed. "The auld laird, Kester's da, started calling it Kester's Meadow, since 'twas a symbol of that betrayal. He declared the peace with the Murray over, and demanded the Murray return the land."

"'Tis verra good land," Weesil explained. "Worth going to war over. And the MacBain is always worrying about our future, aye?"

"Aye, but the MacBains—nae matter how fierce and brave we are—cannae truly mount a war against a clan the size of the Murrays." Pudge shook his head bitterly. "For over two decades now, we've contented ourselves with reaving parties, hit-and-run attacks against the Murray crofts and outposts now spread throughout Kester's Meadow."

Her eyes were wide as she listened. "But those people…."

"Och, we dinnae kill them," Pudge scoffed, "just sort of… acquire some of their more portable wealth. And cause some mischief to them, I cannae lie. I figure 'tis their own fault, for living on our land."

"Kester's Meadow should belong to the MacBains," agreed Weesil without looking up. "If only Ian Murray werenae so stubborn."

If the land really were as fertile as they claimed, Robena could understand why Murray didn't want to give it up. But now….

The sun had sunk behind the trees, and Mook and Giric made plenty of noise as they tromped back into camp, their hair dripping wet as they laughed about something.

The quiet of night began to wrap around them all, but Robena was considering the tale she'd heard.

"He's…. The King wants the feud to end?" she hesitantly offered, thinking of the letter she'd read.

Pudge snorted. "The King doesnae mind a bit of feuding and reaving to keep his warriors in top fighting form! But the Murray has his ear, and the *Murray* wants the feud over. 'Twas his idea to have Kester marry his daughter and end it. He claims he'll gift the meadow to us once the contract's signed. He doesnae need it, no' the way we do, and it'll keep us from bedeviling him."

"Aye, the feud started with a marriage contract, so why no' end it with one?" Auld Gommy mumbled bitterly. "'Twas the Murray's idea, and the King went along with it. Kester learned of the plan last autumn but wanted naught to do with it."

"Remember what he said when he got the word from Murray?" Weesil smirked. "How all it meant was we'd have to double our efforts to relieve them of the takings of Kester's Meadow?"

"Aye, we reaved well last autumn," Pudge agreed. "But Murray must've complained to the King, because the letter he received at Oliphant Castle wasnae subtle."

It is time to marry Lady Elspeth Murray and end this feud.

The bannocks sizzled as Auld Gommy pulled them from the pan and began passing them around. Robena munched hers quietly, considering what she'd learned, as the cook served the stew.

Darkness had settled when she asked the question she'd been half-afraid of. "So...Laird MacBain doesnae want to marry the Murray's auldest daughter?"

Pudge snorted. "He wants naught less. But 'twill help the clan, and the lad is honorable. He'll do what's necessary to secure the clan's future, even if that means taking on a bitch of a wife. Any offspring of a bastard like Murray is likely as entitled and petty as he is."

Spoiled, beautiful, desirable.

And here's Robena, wearing a fake mustache. Her fingers brushed against it as she took another bite of Auld Gommy's stew.

Weesil gestured with his spoon. "We thought there was a lass for him at Oliphant Castle—he was happier there than he'd been in a long while and kept coming up with excuses to stick around."

Nay, he'd been waiting for the King's reply on what to do with the missive Gordon's death had orphaned...hadn't he?

"Aye, the MacBain had definitely taken a fancy to her," crowed Auld Gommy. "Remember how he'd smile when he talked about her? What was her name...?"

"Rohena," offered Weesil.

"Nay, 'twas Rebecca," corrected Auld Gommy.

Robena whispered, "Robena."

"Aye, Robena. He *liked* her. And we're his men." Auld Gommy shrugged as he shoveled a piece of carrot into his mouth. "We like the idea of him settling down with a pretty lass and making a lot of bairns for the future of the clan, eh?"

"Just no' the Murray lass," growled Pudge.

"Nay, I mean the Oliphant one." Auld Gommy sighed. "But our laird is too honorable to take advantage of her, or to let her think they had a chance at a future together."

"Because...." Robena swallowed. "Because he was betrothed to someone else."

"Aye, and he'll marry the lass, even if she's as bad as her da—"

Pudge interrupted the cook. "Because the King commanded it."

"Aye," agreed Weesil, "but also because he's honorable, and he kens this is the best way to stop the feud. He'll marry Murray's daughter for the rest of the MacBains. Once we have the meadow again, we'll no' have to worry about feeding our people."

He's doing it for his clan.

Her stomach churned at the realization, and she dropped her spoon into her bowl. Kester wasn't marrying the Murray lass because she was beautiful or elegant...he was marrying her because doing so would mean his clan was safe.

Our laird is too honorable to take advantage of her, or to let her think they had a chance at a future together.

That's what had happened.

He and his men had stayed at Oliphant Castle for weeks,

and she'd done her best to encourage him, to flirt with him. He'd flirted right back, but until that day in the secret passages —that glorious day, those glorious kisses!—he'd resisted her. Because he knew they had no chance at a future together.

But....

But....

But right here and now, they had a *present* together.

With shaking hands, Robena lowered her bowl to the ground beside her. She swallowed as she tried to work through these thoughts swirling in her head.

He'd been trying to keep her heart safe, but her heart knew what it wanted. It—*she* wanted *him*. And if she couldn't have him forever, then mayhap having him for just a few days would be enough.

"Excuse me," she murmured, pushing herself to her feet and wiping her palms on her kilt.

"Ooh-hoo-hoo!" teased Giric, as he took her spot. "Feeling fancy tonight, Robbie? With the manners, eh?"

"I need...." She guessed where Kester would be. "The lake."

"Aye, lad, I didnae want to say aught to ye," Giric mumbled around a mouthful of stew, "but ye stink."

"All lads stink after a few days in the saddle," assured Weesil. "Even Giric."

"No' me." Auld Gommy stroked his beard fondly. "I'm too auld to stink."

Pudge snorted. "Ye stink enough to choke a goat."

"Well *ye* could choke a bull!" spat the old man in return.

Mook rumbled, "I could choke a bull!"

As Giric muttered, "Aye, ye could," in what sounded like admiration, Weesil quipped, "Ye could choke a snake."

"Nay, that's what Kester's doing all alone by the lake!"

And they all dissolved into guffaws as Robena melted into the shadows, trusting the moon to guide her way.

CHAPTER 5

HE DIDN'T HAVE to turn to know she was there.

Kester stood with one boot foot resting against a large boulder, his back to the woods. He'd been cutting slices from an apple, slowly lifting each to his mouth with his blade to savor the tartness, as he gazed over the moon-bright loch.

He'd have to have been deaf to miss her approach.

"Ye crash through the underbrush like a wounded boar," he said mildly, wiping his dagger on his kilt and tossing the core over his shoulder as he turned. "Ye need to move more quietly."

Sure enough, Robena stood on the edge of the shore, her hands on her hips and her cropped curls full of leaves and twigs.

She shrugged and grinned unrepentantly. "I got lost."

'Twas the mustache. How in damnation was he supposed to know how he felt about her, when she was wearing a mustache? That grin she was giving him never failed to reach down under his kilt and stroke his cock into readiness....

But the mustache made it a confusing erection.

Irritated at himself for even noticing how she smiled, he

scowled as he slammed his dagger into its sheath at his side, opposite the great sword. "How in St. John's name do ye get lost between camp and the loch? 'Tis a straight line!"

She didn't seem bothered by his sharp tone. If anything, her grin grew as she sauntered toward him. "I never claimed to be any good at woodlore or gallivanting at night through the forest."

It should be impossible to saunter erotically while wearing a man's kilt.

Apparently, it wasn't.

"I had a little trouble with what I think was an oak tree," she was saying as she stopped in front of him. "Although mayhap 'twas a pine."

Kester couldn't seem to stop his hand from rising to her temple where sap had glued a cluster of needles to her hair. "Clearly," he murmured drily. "Are ye hurt?"

With her head cocked back, she was smiling up at him now, that mustache big and fluffy on her upper lip. "I'm flattered ye care."

"Of course, I care, lass." It slipped out before he could stop himself. "I mean, ye're under my protection."

"And that's the only reason ye're still touching my hair?"

Oh shite, he was, wasn't he?

Hurriedly, he dropped his hand, but the sap stuck to his fingers, and he cursed himself for his stupidity.

"Why are ye here?" he growled, angry at himself, and at her for not being angry enough at him.

But she just shrugged again. "Auld Gommy made stew."

And that apple wasn't nearly enough. "I'll eat later."

"They're back there telling fine tales about the size of yer cock and claiming ye're out here pleasuring yerself—Are ye aright?" her eyes widened with alarm as he began to choke on his objections.

"*Dinnae* say such things, lass!"

"Why?"

"*Why?*" he repeated incredulously.

She crossed her arms in front of her chest. "Aye. Why can I no' speak about yer cock? 'Tis a subject I'm verra much interested in."

Oh for fook's sake!

"Because…because it isnae seemly!" At a loss, he dragged his hand through his hair and only remembered too late about the sap.

From the direction of her gaze and the way her lips were curled, she'd noticed his sap difficulty.

"I've told ye, Kester, ye needn't worry about my reputation. Out here, I'm Robbie."

With a growl, he pointed one sap-covered finger at her. "And Robbie wouldnae be talking about my cock."

"Why no'?" she challenged. "Yer men have plenty of opinions about yer manhood. They say yer cock is long enough—"

Cursing, he turned away from her, his fingers wrapping around the hilts of his blades, more out of comfort than any real danger.

After a few moments of silence, during which he managed to get his—his—his *everything* under control, she spoke.

"Why do ye care, Kester?" she whispered. "Why does it matter what *I* think—how I *feel*—about ye?"

The moon wasn't quite full, but there were no clouds tonight, and the light reflected peacefully off the surface of the loch. 'Twas small enough there were no waves, just a few ripples the breeze caused across the surface.

Kester inhaled deeply, savoring the Highland scents he loved so much; heather, pine…. Well, that was likely his own hair he was smelling.

Here, and now, with her safely tucked behind him and the reflection of the moon before him, 'twas easier to tell her the truth.

"Because, lass, I suspect I'll care about ye until the day I die."

He heard her exhale quietly.

"Yer men say 'tis the King's wish ye marry Murray's eldest daughter, no' yers."

He had to tread carefully.

"'Tis my wish to have peace for my clan. We're small, and I've been fighting Ian Murray since afore my da died and I became laird. An alliance would provide for my people."

He knew he sounded defeated. He *felt* defeated.

After a long moment, he heard her move closer. When she spoke, she was right behind him. "Ye're a good man, Kester MacBain. A good laird."

He closed his eyes, imagining he could *feel* her heat pressed against his back. "I'm no'." His voice was raw. "If I were a good man, I wouldnae have fallen in love with ye."

Well, shite.

He heard her slow inhale. "Are…are ye sure ye meant to say that out loud already? We're only halfway through."

"Through what?" He opened his eyes to find the vista of the loch hadn't changed.

"Through…." 'Twas easy to imagine her flapping her hands about, in that adorable way of hers. "Through *this*. Our story. Fifty percent seems a bit early."

He turned. "Lass, what *are* ye talking about?"

"I dinnae ken!" she all-but-wailed, her eyes wide. Although he couldn't see it in the dim light, 'twasnae difficult to guess she was panicked. "I came out here to convince ye I dinnae need yer love—"

"Ye dinnae," he declared sharply, reaching for her hands. Shite, his were still sticky, but he squeezed anyhow. "Robena, I'm nae good for ye. Ye *dinnae* need my love."

Her eyes were wide. "But I have it," she whispered.

Well, shite again.

He couldn't deny it, so he said naught.

"Kester…." When she took a deep breath, her shoulders expanded beneath that ridiculous shirt she wore. "Ye've said ye…care for me. I understand now why ye think we couldnae be together, at Oliphant Castle, but…."

When she trailed off, he found himself leaning closer. "But what?" he finally prompted.

She lifted his hands to her lips. Holding his gaze as well as could be expected in the reflected moonlight, she brushed a kiss to his knuckles.

He barely managed to keep from shuddering, and under his kilt, his cock was rock-hard.

"We're no' at Oliphant Castle," she whispered. "We're no' at the Highland Games. Here and now, we're standing alone beside a loch. Nae past, nae future, Kester."

God's Blood, he didn't want to hear this from her.

Well, aye, he *did* want to hear this—wanted it more than his next breath—but each word out of her mouth wore down his resistance.

Be strong.

"I understand yer commitment to yer clan, and to the King." She flattened his hands against her chest and held him there. He could feel her heart pounding against his palms. "But ye have a commitment to yer heart as well."

He swallowed. "Nay."

And of course, she ignored his whisper. "Here and now, Kester MacBain. That's all I'm asking from ye. I want nae commitment, I want nae vows. Just…here and now."

Unbidden, he swayed toward her, his attention on her lips. On her words.

God's Wounds, he wanted to say aye, to agree. But….

"I cannae hurt ye that way."

"Ye'll no' hurt *me*, because I'm asking for it. And nae one else will find out."

She had a point.

What? Nay! Whose side are ye on?

The side of whichever argument was going to allow him to kiss her.

Except....

He swayed closer, then shut his eyes. "Lass?" he croaked out.

"Aye, Kester?" Her voice was the barest whisper, her breath tickling his lips.

"Robena, I...."

She leaned toward him. "Aye!"

And his eyes flashed open. "I cannae take ye seriously with that caterpillar glued to yer upper lip."

Her brows shot up, and he imagined he could see anger in her eyes as she stepped back. But to his surprise, he began to chuckle, and lifted her hand to her lips.

"Ye're right, of course," she declared. Then, "Ow! *Shite*, that hurts!"

He was already reaching for her to help when she—still laughing—twisted away from him.

With a flourish, she placed the hated mustache, glue and all, atop the boulder. Then, afore he could ask what she was doing, Robena bent to unlace her boots.

He folded his arms and watched her, deciding she'd likely explain herself afore she reached her underclothes.

He was wrong.

Instead, he stood there and watched her unbelt her kilt, watched her gather and fold it carefully, the hem of the linen man's shirt she wore falling barely to her thighs, and offering tantalizing glimpses of her arse when she moved. He swallowed, remembering how her bare leg had felt under his palm.

And then she reached for that hem and yanked the whole thing over her head. She placed the shirt carefully on the boulder—moving the mustache atop the folded linen so as not to lose it, huzzah—before Kester could remember how to work his own damn voice.

With her back to him, she began to unwind the length of soft material she'd wrapped around her chest to hold down her small tits.

"Lass?" he finally asked in a choked voice. "What are ye doing?"

She turned just enough to peek over her shoulder at him. "I'm undressing." She was grinning.

"Aye, I can see that."

The twin globes of her arse cheeks were taunting him, and he had to curl his hands into fists to keep from reaching for them—*her*.

As the last loop of linen unwound from her chest, she breathed a sigh of relief. "*Ah.* Ye cannae imagine how *good* that feels. Why would *anyone* want to spend their days confining their breasts that way? Can ye just imagine how ridiculous that would be? To have to wear something so restrictive *every day*, under yer clothes, just to give yer body the silhouette some arbiter of fashion declared necessary?"

She was…words were coming out of her mouth, Kester was almost certain of it. But *what* she was saying exactly…he couldn't seem to focus.

Because she was standing naked before him.

Naked.

On the shores of the loch, the moonlight haloed around her.

Naked.

Bits of her were thrown into shadow, but other—equally important bits—were on display, and his mouth went dry.

Naked.

"Robena?" he croaked.

She smiled. "I'm going to bathe, Kester. I've been riding a horse for what seems like eons, and I'm filthy. Yer men have complimented my 'manly stench', but now I've removed the mustache and am no longer Robbie…."

Turning, she offered him a jaunty wave and sauntered toward the water.

It wasn't until Kester stumbled to stay upright that he realized he was unconsciously following her.

"*Oh!*" She froze when the water lapped against both her feet. "'Tis *cold!*"

He could no more answer her than declare the sun to stop shining.

She shrugged, hugged herself, and then in a sudden flurry of movement, threw herself forward into the water.

"Lass!" he barked as he lunged, yanking himself to a stop only when he saw her rise to the surface.

Water slicked off her shoulders, between the valley of her breasts, and toward the darkness below her navel. Beneath his kilt, his cock throbbed in response.

"Kester?" she called sweetly. "I'm going into deeper water to bathe."

He thought he might've grunted in response.

"And Kester?" Her grin was wide enough he could see it from here. "I cannae swim."

"Ye…cannae swim?"

"Nay! I never learned. I guess I'll just have to trust ye to keep me from drowning."

As she turned away and began that awkward half-swim, half-walk toward deeper water, Kester reached for the clasp of his sword belt.

AS THE WATER closed over her breasts, Robena gave a little shudder which wasn't entirely from the cold.

She wasn't entirely comfortable in the water, aye, but 'twas more than that; the memory of Kester's words did all sorts of funny things to her insides.

He loves me. He said it himself.

The thought *should* make her sad, remind her of the fact a future together would never happen. Instead, though, she focused on the assurance that what she was doing was *right.*

Here and now.

They had here and now to be together.

And judging from the splashes she heard behind her, Kester agreed.

Or he was worried about her drowning.

Either way.

Smiling, she turned toward the shore.

For certes, there was her love, scowling as he splashed toward her. The water had *just* closed around his hips, but that delightful V leading from his abdomen—pointing downward as if to say *Here is the cock! 'Tis right here!*—was visible for a few more steps.

"What are ye staring at?" he barked as he reached her, and they stood awkwardly a few paces apart.

She couldn't afford to be coy. "Ye," she said bluntly. "Ye're a handsome man, Kester MacBain. I've enjoyed riding with ye these last few days, especially since so many of ye seem content to remove yer shirts in the hottest part of the day."

The teasing didn't work, judging from the way his countenance darkened. "And ye were looking at all of us?"

"Och, jealousy isnae fair." *He* was the one on the way to marry another woman. "I only have eyes for ye."

Suiting deeds to words, she allowed her gaze to travel across his shoulders and chest, most of which was still above the water. "And I like what I see. Verra much. Just a pity the water covers the interesting bits."

Instinctively, he glanced down at himself. "What bits?" And

then he rolled his eyes, as if he'd figured out what *bits* she meant.

"Yer arse dimples."

His gaze snapped back to hers, his brows still drawn in. "What?"

He was fun to tease. Robena shifted one foot cautiously along the rocky bottom of the loch, trying to move closer.

"Ye have dimples right above yer buttocks." Since he was still frowning in confusion, she reached for him. "Here." Her hands settled on his hips, then snaked around the back so her fingers rested right below his kidneys. "And here. 'Tis completely normal. A sign of a trim backside."

"I dinnae have arse dimples."

She grinned. "Ye do. Why do ye think I've been staring at yer arse for so long?"

His expression slowly cleared into suspicion. "Is that why ye keep turning on yer horse to stare at me?"

Although 'twas disappointing to release her hold on him, Robena felt in danger of drowning unless she reached higher.

"I cannae see yer arse from that angle. I just like looking at ye."

'Twas a long moment of his gaze flicking from one eye to the other and back, as if looking for the lie, before one corner of his lips finally twitched. "I doubt there's much to look at right now. I dinnae think the cold water's helping. No' with ye looking at me like that."

"Like what?" Goodness, she wasn't at all cold right now.

"Like...." His voice dropped low, as did his eyes. "Like ye need me."

"I do," she whispered, instinctively arching her back so her breasts—which is of course what he was looking at—lifted enough from the water for her nipples to caress the surface.

He made a reverent sound and Robena was *quite* interested

in learning more about *that*...except the movement had thrown her off-balance.

Water was a mysterious place as far as she was concerned; fish shat in it, and 'twas full of slimy things like eels and rocks and shipwrecks. At that moment, her left heel came down on what was either a dead whale or a slimy rock—they felt similar—and she lost her balance.

Thank St. Kelsi he was there to grab her, because otherwise she might've done something outrageous, like get her hair wet.

But since the result was his arms were strong—and warm —against her back, and hers were around his neck, she decided she ought to slip on decomposing blubber more often.

"Robena...." he whispered.

She was pressed against his chest, his hips. And while all of him was delightfully hard, her belly cradled the most *interesting* bit of hardness.

The cold water hadn't affected him one bit.

Here and now.

She could say something coy, but...this is what she'd been hoping for, ever since she'd stumbled out of that wretched forest and seen him posed there on the shoreline, looking like some ancient god.

Nay, she'd been hoping for this long before tonight; since she'd learned the truth about Kester's future—nay, since she'd left Oliphant Castle. Since that time in the secret passageway. Since she'd first been introduced to him.

Since *forever*.

"Kester," she murmured. "I'd verra much like to kiss ye."

There was enough light to see him swallow, but not enough to guess at the emotion in his eyes. She guessed he was debating, and curled her fingers into the hair at the base of his neck.

With a groan of surrender, he pulled her up his body and claimed her lips.

Robena's heart leapt at the same moment her core melted. 'Twas the most delicious sensation, one which stole her breath from her lungs. Or mayhap that was *him*.

Or mayhap she was just afraid of breathing and ruining this perfect moment, with the water lapping against her back and his tongue reminding her what it meant to feel *loved*.

He tasted of apples and joy.

His large, callused hands spread across the bare skin of her back, and the sensation was so unique, she gasped, finally sucking in a lungful of air as his teeth tugged at her lower lip. *That* sent all sorts of interesting sparks across her skin, and she moaned and pressed herself closer to him.

Her own hands refused to be still. Content in the knowledge he would hold her, protect her, she was free to allow her touch to roam across his body, reveling in each touch, each new inch of skin she discovered.

Kissing a naked man was really quite an experience.

His lips trailed hot kisses along her jaw, and she tilted her head to one side to allow him better access as she dragged her fingernails across his scalp. He shuddered and muttered something, his hips flexing forward so the thick length of him pressed against her smooth skin.

She grinned and tipped her head back.

When one of his hands abandoned her back, she had a moment of panic, but only as long as it took for it to settled against the side of her neck. He held her in place as he captured her lips again, and *this* kiss was even better than the first. Possibly because his touch was also roaming.

Where his fingertips brushed against her skin, tiny fires ignited, each spark the mother of five more. She squirmed in his hold, the throbbing in her core growing with each breath....

And then his palm closed around one of her breasts.

She mewled against his lips, arching to thrust herself into his hold, but trying not to break their kiss.

She felt him smile. Felt it all the way into her chest and down to that aching spot between her thighs and back out again.

'Twas really quite a remarkable sensation, to have a man cup one's breast. Especially a breast which had been bound too tight for too long—

Oh.

Whatever she'd been feeling was far eclipsed by what happened to her body when he took her nipple between his thumb and forefinger and *rolled* it.

She went mad.

Her arms tightened around him and, panting, she tried to climb him. As he played with her nipple, she pulled herself higher along his body, instinctively wrapping her legs around his thighs, and then his hips, trying to get closer, closer, closer.

It wasn't until he sucked in a harsh breath and pulled his lips from hers that she realized she'd placed her core—wet, pulsing, *aching*—against the base of his—his *cock.*

With a groan, his forehead dropped to hers. "Lass," he gasped, "Ye're killing me."

But he didn't stop teasing her nipple, and his other hand crept down to her rear end, to cup one cheek and lift her.

Robena decided that she liked the water very much after all.

"No' yet," she gasped. "Ye cannae die yet. No' until—"

His rough palm cupped her breast again, and she broke off with a moan.

As he kissed her once more, she began to rock, to slide up and down his body. Subtly at first, her hips moving in an instinct older than she could guess. Each flex pushed his hardness against her pelvic bone and the bud hidden in her curls, where she *needed* the pressure.

Her left arm tightened around his neck, holding herself in place, while her right hand squirmed down between their bodies.

And before he could figure out what she was doing, her fingers closed around his thickness, marveling at the soft steel.

He stiffened for a moment, muttering a curse against her lips...and then melted as she gently stroked him. She had to lean away from him to have the space, but he didn't fight her. His eyes were closed, an expression something like wonder on his face as her palm brushed against the tip of his cock.

Unable to resist such temptation, she curled her fingers through his hair, pulling his lips back to hers, at the same moment his hand dropped away from her breast.

His fingers brushed against her inner thigh, which was still wrapped around his waist, and she instinctively opened for him. When he brushed along her swollen, needy core, she moaned and dropped her head back.

"God's Wounds, Robena," he rasped. "Ye're so hot. So ready."

"Please," she managed to whisper.

Her fingers were still curled around his hardness, but she couldn't seem to make them move. Her entire being was focused on *his* fingers, and the way they teased, delving in and out of her folds, stroking, caressing.

And then he pushed one callused tip inside her, and she sighed at the sensation. "Aye," she breathed, her eyes closed, her focus on that one delicious invasion. "*More.*"

"No' yet," he murmured, his lips finding her jaw, then her throat. "Soon."

He stroked her, and the pleasure mounted. She was no novice when it came to pleasure, having experimented quite often on herself. But this...! The sensation of the cool water, and his warm body, and each move a surprise....

And his cock, of course. That was an added bonus.

The pad of his thumb found her clitoris and she gasped, her fingers tightening around him.

"Kester!"

Making a sound which might've been a chuckle, he pressed another finger inside her...and her inner muscles contracted *hard*.

"Aye," he groaned, as she tightened around him—in every way. "Come for me, lass."

Well, who was she to refuse such an order?

With another gasp, she flexed against him, feeling her pleasure mounting. He slid his fingers from her just slightly, then pressed into her again as his thumb brushed against her bud of pleasure.

And her pleasure burst white-hot behind her eyes.

She rode him.

There really wasn't any other way to explain it. She rode him, rocking hard against him and his hand, her fingers locked around his cock as her belly and breasts slid along his hardness.

"*Jesu Christo!*" he gasped, his fingers digging into her arse cheek. "Aye, Robena...."

His words devolved into a groan, and dimly, through her own spiraling pleasure, she felt liquid heat spill from the tip of his cock, sliding between their bodies.

They stood—or possibly floated, or melted, or *existed*—like that for a million heartbeats, and also for far too short a time. As her breathing returned to normal, she realized his forehead was pressed against hers once more, his eyes squeezed shut, and his fingers still inside her.

Unable to stop herself, and not wanting to, she brushed her lips against his cheekbone. Then his brow, then his nose. Finally, his eyes opened.

"Robena...."

"If ye apologize, Kester MacBain, I'll smack ye." She flexed her fingers around his cock, which was still pinned between them, and saw him smile.

"Verra well. I was going to say…." He captured her lips in his, this kiss soft, and over too quickly. "Thank ye. Thank ye for giving me this. Here and now."

She swallowed, hating the fact the reminder somehow soured the hum of joy still thrumming through her body. This had been *her* idea. This had been what she wanted.

Here and now.

Forcing a light tone, she smiled. "Thank *ye*, Kester."

Mayhap he'd felt the change in the moment because he blew out a breath and slid his fingers from inside her, loosening his hold on her arse at the same time. She did the same, releasing him, relaxing her legs from around his hips.

He brushed another gentle kiss against her lips, although this one seemed somehow perfunctory. "Shall we bathe?"

That had been the reason she'd goaded him out here, had it not?

"Aye." She turned him toward the shore. "Although mayhap closer to land, eh?"

He sighed as he followed her. "Ye really cannae swim, lass?"

"I never learned. I never needed to."

'Twas likely the smirk she sent over her shoulder which had his lips reluctantly tugging into a grin. "Ye have me."

He'd held her tonight, protected her.

"Aye," she murmured, reaching down to collect a handful of sand to rub into her scalp to clean it. "I have ye."

But no' for long.

CHAPTER 6

KESTER *KNEW* he should feel guilty. So why didn't he?

Because ye enjoyed yerself. Stop with the whining and keep enjoying yerself.

Well, aye.

She was the one who'd made the decision. She was the one who declared herself content with the *here and now*. Robena knew as well as he did that they had no chance for a future together….

But here and now, they had time together.

And *by the saints*, but that had been a remarkable interlude in the loch the other night!

To feel her squeezing him—his fingers, his body, his *cock*—with everything she had. To feel her come apart in his arms as he stroked her to completion….

His mouth watered at the memory.

The fact that weeks' worth of sexual frustration had found release hadn't hurt either.

Kester found himself more relaxed in the days following that night-time bath in the loch. He smiled more, his muscles were more at ease, and he didn't even mind Robena's mustache.

Well, mayhap he *minded* it, but at least he could look at it without cringing.

He could swear it had grown larger and fluffier. Was she adding to it?

"Ye're doing it again."

Her quiet observation jerked his attention sideways where she rode easily beside him. "Doing what?"

"Staring at the mountains and grinning. Well, I say *grinning*, but 'tis more like a vaguely amused look. Verra different from yer normal scowl."

She was teasing him. She'd been teasing him often in the last few days since she'd begun to ride beside him. Mayhap her nearness was the reason for his good mood.

Although the orgasm certainly helped.

But all he said—aye, with a faint smile—was, "I dinnae *normally* scowl. Just since we left yer father's land."

Since he'd received the King's letter.

"Well, now ye're back to scowling."

He realized she was right, and his lips twitched reluctantly.

"There ye are," she murmured, as if welcoming him home.

To his surprise, she nudged her horse closer to his and reached out to place her fingertips lightly against the back of his hand, which rested on his thigh.

As always, her touch sent a flood of warmth, of *rightness* through his limb, and he was unable to stop the instinct to turn his hand over, to twine his fingers through hers.

'Twas awkward, riding beside her while holding her hand, but worth it.

Here and now.

Up ahead, Giric burst into laughter at something Mook said, and slowed his horse until he could ride beside Pudge.

"Did ye hear that, Pudge? Did ye hear what Mook said?"

Pudge was scowling, as usual. As he lifted a skin to his lips, he shook his head, clearly not in the mood to deal with Giric's good cheer. "Pudge isnae here right now. Please leave a message after the beep."

Mook twisted in his saddle. "The fook's a beep?"

"Did he just say *please*?" Weesil whispered in awe at the same time.

Pudge was still staring straight ahead. *"Beeeeeeeep."*

"He beeped!" Mook's frantic look flicked between Pudge and Giric and Auld Gommy. "He beeped! Is he supposed to beep?"

"Should we leave a message?" Weesil hissed.

Auld Gommy rode up on Pudge's other side and waved a wrinkled hand in front of the warrior's face. "Good Lord, he's possessed again!"

Again?

Beside Kester, Robena was chuckling. She pulled her fingers from his and nudged her horse forward. "Nay, he's fine. Just leave a message. He got back to me last time."

Mook was shaking his head. "That *is* Pudge! I can see him! That's Pudge right there!"

But Giric, looking uncertain, leaned closer to the stoic man and cleared his throat. "Ho, Pudge? Um…'tis Giric. I wanted to tell ye Mook's joke. When ye have a chance, get back to me, aright?"

Without glancing over, Pudge nodded solemnly. "Beep."

Giric looked relieved—and still confused—when he sat back in his saddle. His horse had slowed enough to allow Robena to catch up with him.

"He'll get back to ye, dinnae fash."

"Do I have to beep at him?"

She grinned. "Nay, no' unless ye want to."

The handsome man was staring at her, his attention obviously diverted. "Och, lad, ye *must* tell me how ye get yer mustache so luxurious! I find myself jealous of a wee stripling!"

"Glue."

"What?"

Robena shook her head. "Never mind. 'Tis a family secret."

And Kester, unable to help himself, began to chuckle.

Weesil glanced over his shoulder and grinned at his laird, and Kester wondered how worried they'd all been about his doldrums. Well, they'd have to get used to it; once he married Murray's daughter, they'd learn exactly how depressed a man could—

Och, nay, dinnae dwell on the future, ye arse. Here and now.

Aye. Here and now, Robena made him happy, even if he hadn't the chance to sneak her away for more kisses. He knew that was all they could share, not with her reputation at stake. Unless she wanted to bathe again. Then he'd have no choice but to go in the loch after her.

Right.

"Laddie!" called Auld Gommy. "How about a song?"

Robena was already reaching for her lute—which she'd taken to strapping to the saddle without wrapping since the men enjoyed her playing so much—when she asked, "Which one?"

"Och, make up a new one for us!"

Her fingers plucked out a succession of soft, cheerful notes. "About what?"

"About the story Mook just told!" hooted Giric. "Tell it again!"

The large man smiled hugely over his shoulder. "Ye remember, Auld Gommy? 'Twas the time ye were napping under that bush—"

"This again?" snapped the old man. "I was *resting my eyes!*"

"And I had to take a piss, aye?" chortled Mook. "Only I didnae ken ye were under there!"

Kester shook his head, a smile tugging at his lips. He remembered this, aye, and how angry Auld Gommy had been.

"Robbie!" Mook called, hardly able to breathe, he was laughing so hard, "Robbie, ye should've seen the way—the way Auld Gommy rose up out of that bush!"

Giric was doubled over with laughter, while Weesil snickered. Pudge, ignoring them all, kicked his horse into a trot to take point, while the others clustered around Robena's animal.

She strummed the lute, making the notes loud enough to gain attention. "I think I have an idea where this is going."

"I've changed my mind, Robbie lad," grumbled Auld Gommy. "I dinnae want to hear a song after all."

"Well, *I* do!" hooted Giric.

Robena frowned thoughtfully, her lips moving silently as she strummed. Finally, her face broke into a smile.

Kester found himself urging his horse closer to hear her words.

She began to hum, a spritely little tune which matched the notes she was playing. Then:

"In the merry month of May—"

"Och, *nay!*" interrupted Auld Gommy, frantically shaking his head. "Robbie, lad, ye *cannae* start a good song with 'in the merry month of May'! Everyone kens that!"

From ahead, Mook rumbled, "'Twas September, I think."

"Aye, ye dobber, but ye cannae rhyme aught with September," Weesil pointed out.

Mook frowned. "September rhymes with *remember.*"

Weesil glanced, wide-eyed, at Giric. "Is he right?"

Giric grinned hugely. "He's right. Good work, Mook!"

"I think I could rhyme January with 'wee'," mused Robena,

her fingers plucking at the strings again. "Any chance 'twas January?"

"January's too cold to take a piss outdoors," snapped Auld Gommy. "What kind of lad are ye, ye dinnae ken that sort of thing?"

Kester began to chuckle.

"Oooh," Robena teased. "So ye only piss indoors all winter?"

"When ye get to be my age, Robbie, ye're afraid a bit of cold might freeze yer willie!"

"Who's Willie again?" asked a confused Mook

With a lewd gesture toward his crotch, Giric bragged, "Have to be more than a *bit* to freeze *mine*, auld man!"

This time, even Robena laughed.

Kester found himself shaking his head in bemusement. She was a *lady*. A lady born and raised in a castle, the daughter of a laird, trained in the fine arts of music and singing and embroidery.

Yet here she was, paying no mind to what things *should* be, laughing with his men about their cocks.

"*In the merry month of January—*"

"*Nay!*" interrupted Auld Gommy with a scowl. "Anytime a song starts with *in the merry month*, we ken it'll be a *folk song.*" He spat out the words. "We want something *real*, something that stirs our blood! Give us a *ballad*, Robbie!"

She didn't seem concerned with the feedback. "Ye want a ballad about pissing on each other?"

The men agreed whole-heartedly.

Grinning, she began to hum thoughtfully once more. Then:
"Every man here and there
Kens one important fact;
When camping in the wilds,
Ye want a fire at yer back.

But the circle of the firelight
Only goes so far.
Outside of that, a man can see
The shadows, moon, and stars.
For a bit of privacy and such,
That's where ye want to be;
And that is why I stepped outside
For a little bit of a wee."

As the men broke into hoots of approval and laughter, Robena raised her voice.

"How was I to possibly ken
Outside that bit of light
Was where my friend Auld Gommy
Lay his head down for the night?
The kind of tree's important,
Ye cannae deny me this.
But I could dally nae longer;
I had to take a piss."

Kester nearly choked on his laughter, to hear the word "piss" out of the mouth of the woman he loved. Of course, that mouth was currently topped by a fake mustache, so there was no telling what she might do.

She was grinning hugely when she continued the song.

"My shoulders wide, my legs are strong;
Like a castle I'm built.
So it took some time for me to find
And raise the hem of my kilt.
But I stood afore that mighty bush
And let loose a mighty stream...
Which became verra awkward
To be interrupted by a scream.
Auld Gommy rolled from beneath that bush,
Flailing at his hair.

But I couldnae stop my mighty piss,
Even if I'd had a care."
Weesil fell off his horse, he was laughing so hard.

There were tears running down Giric's cheeks as he pointed to his fallen comrade. "Compose a song about *him* next, Robbie! The dobber fell off his horse!"

Mook was tapping his thigh happily, as if he was only paying attention to the music, and Auld Gommy was hooting with laughter, despite being the butt of the joke.

Even dour Pudge was wearing a smile.

Kester, still chuckling, urged his horse up beside his old friend's. "The song was funny, aye?"

Pudge dropped his chin in acknowledgement, before taking a swig from his skin. "Aye," he drawled as he wiped his mouth with the back of his hand. "The lass is clever, I'll give her that."

It took a moment for his words to sink in, but then Kester sent him a sharp look. Pudge shrugged.

"The rest might be blind, but a mustache dinnae fool me. She's the lass ye were mooning over at Oliphant Castle, is she no'?"

Kester debated how to answer, especially with his old friend watching him so shrewdly. Finally, he looked away. "I thought…we might've had a chance at a future."

"And now she's willing to wear a mustache to go chasing after ye, Laird."

"Nay!" Kester glanced at the others, still laughing. "She's… she's attending the piping competition."

Pudge hummed, his finger tapping idly against his thigh as they rode on, leaving the others to follow. "She's talented, as I said. So, she pretends to be a lad for that reason? No' because she wanted to be with ye?"

Here and now.

Kester twisted slightly in the saddle and met Robena's eyes. Hers were twinkling merrily, clearly amused at how her song had been received.

When they'd set out on this journey, he'd thought her angry at him. Mayhap she *was*, until she learned the truth of his impending marriage, and how little he wanted it. Until he accidentally confessed his love to her.

But now…. "I'm…no' certain," he confessed.

"Have ye asked her?"

Leave it to Pudge to cut to the heart of the matter. "She says she's content with…what I can give her. Here and now. She understands we cannae have a future together."

"Well, Laird," Pudge growled, slamming his fist into Kester's shoulder, "Ye should make the best of what time together ye *do* have."

And that was all the grizzled warrior said before he clucked at his horse and left Kester alone with his thoughts.

Or…mostly alone. Behind him, his men were still guffawing good-naturedly, and after a while, Robbie appeared beside him.

He wanted to take her hand again. Wanted to pull her off her horse, tug off the ridiculous mustache, and sit her on his lap where he could kiss her neck and play with her tits with his free hand. The thought had his cock twitching beneath his kilt.

Unfortunately, *here and now* she was Robbie, and his men were watching. He didn't want them to guess he was in love with a scrawny lad who possessed the remarkable ability to grow a mustache.

"Ye were smiling there for a moment," she murmured.

"So I was." His lips curled ruefully. "I was thinking what I wanted to do to ye."

"Mmm, I like the sound of that." She shot him a grin. "*I* was admiring yer arse dimples."

Unbidden, his finger dropped to his lower back, searching for the dimples she claimed he had on either side of his spine.

Her laughter stopped him, and he found himself chuckling and shaking his head.

"Ye're a joy, Robena," he murmured.

"I am." She winked at him. "Wait 'til ye hear my next song!"

THAT EVENING they made camp beside a stream which ran into a copse of trees. The men were at ease, knowing they were deep within an ally's land, although Kester made certain they were divided into the usual watches.

Auld Gommy was roasting a brace of hares Giric had taken with his bow, and the mood was light.

"Ye ken, Laird," Weesil said suddenly, his attention on oiling his blades. "We're no' so far from Murray land."

"Are we going in circles, then?" rumbled Mook. "We've been traveling for days and we left the Murrays back home, I thought."

"Aye, ye big dobber." Giric smiled as he tossed the big man an apple. "But Weesil's talking about the *other* side of their land. We've been forced to travel around it, but we're coming up on the other side of the Murrays."

"Oooh." Mook bit into the apple. "So, they dinnae ken about us over here?" he asked as he chewed.

Auld Gommy's head popped up wearing a wickedly contemplative grin, and Giric glanced at Weesil, his brows raised.

"He's right," Weesil murmured. "They wouldnae be expecting us over here."

Giric fair beamed excitement when he turned to Kester. "What about it, laird? We could cause some mischief to those bastards, make 'em remember us. 'Tis petty, aye, but 'twould be nice."

Kester, who was resting with his back to a boulder as he idly flipped his dagger from one hand to the other, glanced at Robena. She was either totally engrossed in her lute or she was doing a good impression of paying them no attention.

Auld Gommy shook a spoon at them. "That bastard Murray deserves all the trouble we can offer him, Laird! That alliance isnae final until ye sign the marriage contract with Lady Elspeth! Let us take some revenge for ye, eh?"

Robena hunched further over her instrument. Kester wished he could see her expression, although he suspected from the tightness in her shoulders that it wouldn't be pretty.

Slowly, he nodded. "I cannae deny 'twould be nice."

"Just a bit of fun, Laird," Weesil wheedled, "afore ye're shackled to a wife ye dinnae want."

"Puir bastard," muttered Giric.

Mook crunched on the apple. "Better him than us."

Kester shrugged, unable to deny the appeal of one more chance to make Murray pay. Because of that old bastard, Kester was forced to choose between what was best for his clan and what felt best for *himself*. He knew he would do what his clan needed…but that didn't mean he had to be happy about it.

"I'll consider it, aright?"

Giric hooted and punched the air. "The day after next, we'll be alongside their land! Let's come up with some ideas, lads!"

Robena's head had jerked up at Giric's announcement. "Then…we're so close to the Games?"

She knew her maps. Kester shouldn't be surprised. "Aye, la —lad. Only a few more days' travel and we'll be there."

'Twas impossible to keep a note of defeat from his tone. Let his men think 'twas because he dreaded marriage to Lady

Elspeth… When Robena met his gaze, he knew she understood the truth.

Their *here and now* would only last a few more days.

A new voice drifted from the shadows. "Only a few more days until the piping competitions."

'Twas Pudge, who'd been scouting for places to stand watch. Now he melted into the firelight, holding Robena's gaze. "Ye think ye have a shot at winning, lad?"

Kester watched Robena swallow then nod.

"Well…." Pudge folded his arms and leaned his hip against the same boulder. "We havenae heard ye pipe yet. We ken ye're skilled with yer fingers and voice, but can ye pipe?"

"Aye, Robbie!" Giric nudged her with his boot. "Let us hear some piping!"

She swallowed again, glancing around the circle of firelight at each of the men. Her gaze landed on Kester and hesitated. Finally, she nodded and stood.

As the men called out encouragement and mockery, she carefully unwrapped her pipes from their bundle. 'Twas obvious she cared deeply for them.

With a strong stance, she settled back on her heels beside the cheerful fire, took a deep breath, inflated the bag….

And the notes swept around their little camp.

The song was low and soft and haunting. Something a man could listen to as he drank quietly on a winter's eve. 'Twas easy to imagine the mournful tune as a dirge, or mayhap a lament for times gone by.

The men sat or stood silently, their attention on the auburn-haired, mustached beauty who played with her eyes closed.

The song changed, wrapping them in a beat—which should be impossible with only the pipes and no accompaniment. Kester saw horses thundering into battle, and comrades lost, and swords put aside. He saw a life growing old, mourning what was gone, disappointment at chances missed.

Across the circle, Mook dropped his head to his forearms. Auld Gommy stared at the fire, blinking fiercely. Weesil and Giric watched with mouths agape as Robena swept them all into another sound, this one more celebratory.

This sound was for dancing and loving and laughter, a pretty lass on a cold night, and all the ale one could drink. 'Twas joy and hope and the laughter of bairns, of knowing your life was as good as you could hope, and that you were safe.

It hurt just as much as the mournful dirge.

Because Robena had opened her eyes. She'd opened her eyes and looked right at him, and Kester *knew* this song was for him. They all were.

Because their time together was nearly over.

When Robena finally blew her last note, silence descended over the circle of firelight.

There were one or two sniffs from Mook, and someone cleared his throat once, twice.

And then Pudge took a deep breath. "Aye, Robbie," he finally said, exhaling. "I think ye might just win."

"Where'd ye learn to play like that?" Giric whispered, eyes still wide.

Robena's fingers trailed over the pipes, her chin ducked low, as if she would rather still be playing. "I-I practiced atop the battlements," she confessed. "Where I couldnae bother anyone."

The mystery of the ghostly piper is solved, then.

Kester nodded. "Ye have a real talent, la-lad." His throat felt thick and his eyes burned.

She ducked her head as she turned away. "Thank ye. Ex-excuse me."

When she dropped her pipes near her saddle, 'twas with

less care than they'd been given before. Kester could tell she was hurting and pushed himself to his feet, staring after her as she escaped into the darkness, before he realized what he was doing.

He took a step toward the woods where she'd disappeared, and then Pudge was beside him.

"She'll follow the stream," he murmured, low enough the others wouldn't hear him. "She's shite at woodlore."

Kester nodded agreement and slipped away. Behind him, he heard Weesil ask, "Where's the laird gone?" and Mook rumbled, "Mayhap he has to piss."

But Pudge growled, "He's bucking up the lad. 'Twas some beautiful piping, ye have to admit."

The firelight and the sounds of the men faded behind Kester as he followed first the murmurs of the babbling brook, and then the thuds of some large, possibly berserk animal crashed through the underbrush ahead.

His lips twitched. She could ride a horse, but Robena *was* shite in the woods.

He caught up to her in a little clearing, where she stood with her face tilted back as if admiring the stars. The moonlight glinted off the tears on her cheeks.

Kester didn't say anything, but when he stopped beside her and took her hand, she clasped it as if it were a rope and she was drowning. Which, given she swam about as well as she crept through the woods, was saying a lot.

After a long while, Kester figured he ought to say something. "Ye're going to win."

She sniffed and closed her eyes. "I dinnae ken."

"I do," he vowed quietly. "Ye're remarkable, Robena Oliphant."

In so many ways.

Slowly, she turned to face him. Her lips curled slightly, sadly, mockingly. "I wish it were enough."

I do as well, lass.

With a muttered curse, he pulled her into his arms, and claimed her lips with his. Her arms snaked around his back as he tugged on her hair to encourage her to open for him.

There in the moonlight, they kissed.

And it wasn't enough, but it would have to be.

Here and now.

'Twas all they had.

CHAPTER 7

Robena couldn't decide if she hated herself or not. It had been *her* idea to embrace the short time she had with Kester, and she was glad for that opportunity.

But that joy was tempered by what she could only describe as a constant state of impending doom as they got closer and closer to their destination.

The night she piped for the men, she and Kester spent an hour in the woods, holding one another and talking. And kissing. The kissing was nice.

But again, 'twas sweetness mixed with sorrow. The knowledge that this was all they could *ever* have, and even this would be over soon.

She'd cried and laughed, and then—exhausted—fallen asleep in his arms.

They'd awoken before dawn; him wrapped in his plaid, and her wrapped in him.

And she'd had to bite her tongue to keep from crying again, because until she'd experienced it, she hadn't realized how much she wanted to awake *every* day like this.

The next night was much the same, although she had no

idea what excuse he offered to his men when he followed her into the woods after her piping had once again moved her to tears.

She couldn't help her choice of music; her songs were a reflection of her heart.

But now they were only two days from the Games and had made their excursion onto Murray land.

"Should we be just...sitting around like this?" she asked, pacing around the clearing in the woods. The horses were still saddled but had been set loose to drink from the creek. "What if we're discovered?"

"We'll no' be discovered," muttered Giric, who lay on his back with his hands folded over his stomach, his eyes closed. "The laird and Weesil will warn us afore that happens."

"Aye, laddie." Auld Gommy was picking at his teeth with a dagger. "They're scouting—no' just for opportunity, but trouble as well. And besides, Pudge has the best ears of any MacBain warrior."

When she glanced at the grizzled veteran, who stood with his arms across his chest and frown on his face, he shrugged. "'Tis true," he admitted. "And the horses will no' let us be ambushed."

"There's nae one out here," Mook explained. "Nae one will ken we're here until 'tis too late."

Tis too late.

She shuddered as the simple statement called to mind horrors.

When the men had first suggested a raid on Murray land, it had seemed a lark. She hadn't objected because, well...she would gladly accept any excuse to prolong this journey a day or two.

But now...she worried what she'd agreed to participate in.

"Are ye...what are ye planning on doing?"

She liked these men, and thought *Are ye planning on raping and murdering innocents?* sounded a little too accusatory.

Pudge snorted quietly. "Worried, Robbie?"

Mook grinned. "'Tis the Murrays who should be worried! When Widowmaker is unsheathed, they'll ken it!"

"Widow…maker?" whispered Robena, eyes wide.

"'Tis the name of his great bloody weapon," muttered Giric from his spot on the ground.

"Aye!" Mook gestured gleefully at the front of his kilt. "'Tis huge—"

"*No' yer cock,*" interrupted the handsome man, without opening his eyes.

Robena glanced between the two men, then at the large blade hanging from Mook's hip. "Yer sword is named Widowmaker?" she guessed.

Auld Gommy waved the dagger he'd been using for oral hygiene. "All great warriors name their blades, lads. Or bows, in Giric's case."

"Windsong," Giric announced proudly with a grin as he pushed himself up on his elbows. "It sends arrows straight and true, whistling a deadly song."

"This one is Lefty," Auld Gommy announced proudly, sticking the tip of his dagger back between his teeth and patting his hip. "And this is Righty."

"That sounds…easy to remember," she acknowledged weakly. When she glanced at Pudge, he raised his brow in challenge.

"Does yer blade have a name?" she ventured.

His frown didn't change. "Of course no'. 'Tis silly to name a tool. Widowmaker," he snorted dismissively.

"Pudge hasnae named his sword, Robbie," Giric announced, "but the Murrays call it *The Scowling Menace.*"

As Mook's horse wandered over, she coughed to hide her

chuckle. "That is…fitting. And Weesil? He has so many daggers…?"

"Aye, and every one of them is called Mortal Peril," Auld Gommy explained. "He says 'tis easier to keep track of them that way."

Well, that made sense. "And Kest—I mean, Laird MacBain?" She knew he wore a long sword at his hip and a matching dagger. Did they have names?

Grinning, Giric lowered his voice, as if imparting a great secret. "His dagger is called Blooddrinker."

Oh. Her eyes widened, having trouble reconciling such a bloodthirsty image with the man she knew. "And his sword?" she whispered.

Giric, Auld Gommy, and Mook all answered together, in an awestruck tone: "Karen."

She blinked. "That—*Karen?* He named his sword *Karen?* What does that signify?" she asked Pudge.

The older man shrugged. "'Tis just a collection of syllables, Robbie. It doesnae have to mean aught."

"Nay, but it strikes fear into the hearts of men," whispered Giric gleefully.

"Aye!" Mook nudged his horse out of the way with an open palm. "And into their spleens as well!"

The handsome man frowned at his friend. "It strikes fear into the hearts of spleens?"

"Nay, it strikes fear into the spleens of men!"

Auld Gommy muttered something about idiots, and Robena rubbed her sweaty palms along her plaid-covered thighs for the three-dozenth time that morning.

"I—I dinnae have a weapon."

"Do ye want one?" Giric asked eagerly, rolling to his feet. "Weesil will lend ye a blade! Or I could cut ye a stout oak branch and ye can bash some heads!"

She grew queasy at the thought, but help came from an unexpected source.

"Leave him alone," Pudge announced. "Our Robbie is a bard, and he's coming along to learn the story of today, no' fight."

As Giric and Mook teased her, she swallowed and nodded, grateful. Aye, she could handle *watching*, could she not?

What if ye dinnae like what ye see?

"So, what do ye think the plan will be?" Giric asked idly.

Auld Gommy was wiping his dagger on his shirt. "It'll depend what the laird learns. Do ye remember last—nay, two years ago? That crofter with the sweet-looking daughter?"

Giric chuckled knowingly, and Robena's stomach flipped over again. How could these men, whose company she enjoyed, laugh about *rape*?

Mook's horse stamped one of its front feet and the big man smiled. "We showed him, for certes."

St. Kelsi, forgive them.

Auld Gommy was grinning. "Aye, likely took him 'til winter to get his doors hung back up proper!"

As the rest of them laughed, Robena's dread slowly turned to confusion. "Doors?" she whispered.

Mook's horse lowered itself to its knees.

"Aye, doors!" Auld Gommy guffawed. "Mook stole all the pins from 'em, see? So, no' only could they no' *shut* the doors, the puir bastard would have to have a smith make an entire new set afore he could fix them proper!"

The horse flopped over on its side, and not a single one of them seemed to care.

Robena's wide-eyed gaze flipped between the men. "What do ye mean, *ye took the pins?*"

"Och, are ye deaf, lad?" Giric shook his head with a smile. "The MacBain smith was grateful for the metal—he forged them into scythes for the harvest, remember? That was the same raid where we plucked all the herbs from the crofter's garden and gave them to our healer."

"Nay, 'twas a different one, earlier in the season," Pudge corrected drily. "*That* raid we shaved the puir bastard's horse's tail, remember, and the laird had it fashioned into a wig for the chandler's wife, who was so upset about losing her hair."

"Och, aye! The crofter thought we were going to kill his beastie! He was so scared he was ready to shite himself!" Giric guffawed, slapping at his thigh. "And then we sheared his sheep!"

Robena hesitated. "Ye...stole his sheep?" There hadn't been any rape and murder?

But Auld Gommy shook his head. "Nay, lad, we just sheared them. A few weeks early! Stole all the wool and it kept the MacBains warm all winter long!"

Pudge offered, "We've stolen goats afore, though. Do ye ken how hard 'tis to herd goats?"

"Impossible!" hooted Giric.

"Only about half of them made it back to restock our herds," Auld Gommy corrected. "The rest wandered off, because Mook is shite at keeping track of goats. Remember the time we plucked the chickens?"

"Och, aye, and stuffed the feathers into pillows." Pudge finally cracked a smile. "And it turned out Weesil was allergic to chicken feathers."

The rest of the men roared with laughter and Robena slowly sank onto a boulder.

Plucking chickens? Stealing wool? *Shaving a horse?*

"That's.... Ye just cause mischief?" she clarified weakly.

Giric slapped her back, causing her to pitch forward. "Do we ever! We've made life hell for the Murrays who dare to claim Kester's Meadow as their own! And we will until it belongs to the MacBains once more!"

As it will once Kester marries Lady Elspeth.

Robena didn't miss the fact that every bit of mischief these men caused somehow benefitted the MacBains.

"Leave the lad alone," admonished Pudge. "Robbie expected us to be murdering people, stealing cattle, and burning crops, I expect."

She swallowed, and when all the men turned astonished gazes at her, managed a weak shrug. "Ye said *reaving*."

"Aye!" Giric slammed a palm to his chest. "No' *murdering*!"

Mook nudged his horse with his boot, sounding forlorn when he asked, "What would I do with cattle? I cannae even keep *one* animal moving."

Auld Gommy spat. "And burning crops is a waste of food *and* fire."

"Kester's Meadow will be ours again soon," Pudge pointed out. "'Twould be stupid to burn it or damage the herds it supports."

"Honestly, lad, who *raised ye*?" Auld Gommy shook his head in despair. "Ye have a horrible definition of mischief."

Or they had a horrible definition of *reaving*.

But they'd become her friends and she'd hurt them, so she offered a sincere look when she said, "I'm sorry I offended ye. Thank ye for taking the time to explain."

Auld Gommy sniffed haughtily and pushed himself to his feet. "Well, ye apologize prettily, I'll give ye that."

Pudge held up his hand for silence. "The laird's returning. I recognize those hoofbeats."

Sure enough, a few minutes later Kester and Weesil rode into their clearing. Their legs, and most of their horses, were dripping wet. The man she loved was wearing an easy smile, and 'twas easy to imagine him already planning their *mischief*.

"What'd ye learn, laird?" Giric called.

"Plenty of pickings, lads!" Kester swung down. "All is well here?"

Giric jerked a thumb at Mook who was crouched over his mount. "Ignore the beastie. He's no' dead, just lazy."

"Who, Mook?" asked Weesil, sliding out of his saddle as well.

"No' Mook, the hor—*och*, ye're teasing." Giric rolled his eyes. "Are ye going to tell us the plan, or do we have to drag it out of ye?"

Weesil shot a glance around the circle of men, all of whom had clustered around, with the exception of Robena. "I'll let the laird explain, assuming we can drag Robbie away from his nice soft rock."

"'Tis a boulder," she mumbled. "And I'm just observing this raid. No' participating."

"He's right," Kester declared with a nod. "I'll no' have Robbie placed in danger." When more than one of his men raised a brow at that declaration, he didn't do anything as crass as fluster, but *did* clear his throat. "The lad is competing in a few days. We cannae risk his future."

"Aright," growled Pudge. "What's the plan?"

Kester jerked his attention to Weesil, then moved across the clearing. As the rest of the men shifted their attention to the smaller man, Kester crossed his arms and leaned his hip against the boulder where Robena sat.

Weesil's grin was much broader than one she normally saw on the small man. "Ye remember the patch of blackberries we passed? We found a shepherd's hut. There's two men, but we were able to sneak in. There's some supplies there, an empty vat and…." He gestured them all to lean in. "A jug of vinegar!" he finished triumphantly.

Pudge rolled his eyes as Giric whooped happily. "Sheep again, aye?"

"What?" rumbled Mook.

Auld Gommy was chuckling. "If we have enough time with

the beasties, we can ruin their market sales this autumn! Gray wool is harder to sell!"

"Even better," Kester interrupted with a boyish grin. "If they have to take gray wool to market, *we* can buy it at a reduced price. Our people will be warm—for cheap!—this winter. Assuming they dinnae all mind wearing gray."

"We'll ruin 'em with *capitalism!*" cackled Auld Gommy.

Mook was glancing back and forth. "*What?*"

"I'm thinking 'twill take two groups—one to gather the berries and make the dye, and one to round up the sheep," Kester explained. "I'll take Pudge and Auld Gommy—since the pair of ye are shite with live animals—and we'll start with the—"

"What are ye talking about?" demanded Mook.

Giric took pity on him and patted the large man's upper arm. "We're dyeing the sheep."

"We're killing sheep?" Mook sounded aghast and Robena turned her head to hide her snort of laughter.

"Nay, ye dumb shite," growled Pudge. "*Dyeing* 'em."

"I dinnae want to make sheep die!" wailed the large man.

Kester didn't bother hiding his smile when he called out, "Coloring their wool, Mook. That's the plan."

"Och, then why did ye no' *start* with that?" Mook shook his head at Pudge. "Going on about killing puir wee beasties."

"This from the man who can eat a side of mutton by himself," murmured Kester, and Robena pressed her palm to her mouth—and her mustache—to hide her chortles.

"The shepherds will be a problem," Giric mused. "Especially since we'll need to be there a while."

Weesil nodded. "We'll need a distraction."

Auld Gommy hopped to his feet, beaming. "Leave it to me, lads! I'll have those two Murrays so confused they won't ken what's happening!"

"And how will ye do that, auld man?" growled Pudge. "Cook for them?"

The old man ignored the insult. Instead, he underwent a transformation that left Robena agape.

Auld Gommy pulled himself up to his full height, thrusting his shoulders back as he pursed his lips at Pudge. He knocked his knees together and grabbed a hold of his kilt in both hands, swinging it back and forth around his thighs.

"Tee-hee," he cooed in a high-pitched tone. "Ye're such a braw pair of men. Are ye brothers? Mayhap we can find a way to pass the time, lads?"

Kester sputtered on his laughter while Giric hooted.

"I'm in love," murmured Mook, awe-struck.

Pudge shook his head and said drily, "Ye have a beard, ye auld fooker. 'Tis down to yer waist!"

In that same high-pitched voice, squeezed through his pursed lips, Auld Gommy declared, "I'll plait some flowers in it. They'll never notice!"

Although Kester and Giric were still laughing, Weesil patted the air, gesturing for silence. "'Tis a good idea, actually. The guards would be definitely distracted, and Auld Gommy could get 'em with their kilts up and tie them up."

"Nae one will ever believe *that* is a lass!" declared Pudge hotly, stabbing his finger at the old man who was still making kissing noises.

Robena was surprised to hear herself volunteering. "I'll do it." She pushed herself off the rock and cleared her throat. "I could pass as a lass."

As the men stared, Kester was the first to object. "Nay. Absolutely no'."

From the sincerity of his tone, she guessed his issue was with the thought of her participating at all.

But Weesil snorted and shook his head. "Ye couldnae pass as a lass, Robbie. No' with that lovely mustache."

The mustache was the issue? "But Auld Gommy's beard—" she began, only to be interrupted by the old man, whose voice had returned to normal.

"Nae offense, laddie, but there are certain *tells* a man looks for in a lass, ye ken? The way she stands, the way she plays with her hair." He winked flirtatiously while twirling a strand of his beard around one finger. "See? Ye dinnae do any of that, and ye dinnae *sound* like a lass."

Robena opened her mouth but couldn't think of a single response.

"Besides, the mustache," pointed out Auld Gommy smugly.

"I could…shave?" She wasn't certain why she continued to offer suggestions, especially when the responses of the men around the circle ranged from shock to outrage.

"*Shave* that mustache?" Giric was shaking his head forcefully. "'Twould be a crime against nature!"

"Are ye daft, lad?" murmured Weesil as Mook announced, "Auld Gommy's prettier."

Pudge just raised a brow at her, his eyes twinkling with some emotion she couldn't identify.

Beside her, Kester muttered, "*Jesu Christo.*" He shook his head.

"Nay, lad," Weesil announced with conviction. "Thank ye for yer volunteering, but we'll use Auld Gommy this time. Mayhap when ye're aulder ye'll make a more convincing lass. Now, we're all going to have to cross the river first. 'Twas no' too deep, but is running fast."

As he squatted to draw a map in the dirt and the men nudged aside one of Mook's horse's legs to gather closer, Kester shifted his weight so he was closer to her.

"Are ye certain ye dinnae mind joining us?" he murmured. "I'll stay behind with ye, if ye're uncomfortable."

"Ye're really just planning on dyeing the sheep's wool?"

That *was* mischief, and she found herself grinning at the thought.

Kester shrugged, his attention still on the men, but a boyish grin on his lips. "Dyeing the *sheep*. 'Tis the fun of it, ye ken."

She could understand why Laird Murray wanted to make peace with this man. The MacBain led a fine band of warriors, but they were an *annoyance*. As Pudge had pointed out, they *could* do much worse, but why would they if they planned on claiming the land for themselves?

Was it any wonder her smile was a bit sad when she told the man she loved, "I'll no' deny ye one last time to make trouble for Laird Murray, Kester. As ye said, it'll be fun."

Something flickered in his blue eyes, and he reached for her…only to stop himself and scrub his hands across his face as if he'd meant to do that all along.

The men were beginning to mount up, calling taunts and instructions back and forth. Mook was cajoling his horse into gaining its feet, and Giric gave Auld Gommy a lift into the saddle.

Kester blew out a breath. "Aye, *Robbie*," he finally said without looking at her. "Let us enjoy what time we have, eh?"

'Twas…*interesting*, riding in the midst of what she could only call a war party. Aye, she knew the MacBains weren't heading to battle—not really. But they were silent and swift, their horses well-trained and their senses on high alert.

Even Auld Gommy, who was practicing his lines—"*Och, sirrah, what strong arms ye have!* Nay, higher. *What strong arms ye have! Can I touch them? Teehee.*"—did so under his breath. The rest of them were focused on their surroundings, more than a few hands resting on the hilts of swords.

They met with no Murrays on the way to the river.

Robena could hear the rushing water, but couldn't see it, when Pudge lifted a fist, calling for a halt. She was boxed in on all sides by the warriors, as if by unspoken agreement to protect the youngest of their party.

After at least five minutes of peering out from the covering shadows of their forest, the grizzled veteran made a sweeping gesture with his hand to catch their attention. He held up three fingers, then knocked his fists against each other then pointed at his left eye. He gave one firm nod, tugged on his left earlobe, then tapped his left thumb against the inside of his right wrist. Finally, he placed his two fists beside each other, and made a breaking motion.

They stared at him.

Pudge stared back expectantly.

Finally, Mook whispered, "*What?*"

His brows lowering and his countenance darkening, Pudge repeated the entire pantomime, each motion more abrupt, angrier.

When he was through the second time, Mook glanced at Robena and shrugged. "I dinnae understand."

In a bored voice, Giric—who was sorting through his quiver—said loudly, "He wants us to cross the river two by two and stand watch for the others."

"Aye," hissed Pudge. "Only *silently*."

"Oooh," Mook rumbled. "Well, why did ye no' say that?"

Kester and Weesil crossed first since they'd done it before. Pudge was in charge of timing the rest of their crossings. When the first pair reached the opposite side—the tops of their saddles hadn't even touched the water—Kester swung down and tossed his reins to Weesil, who led the two horses to cover.

Kester crouched on the riverbank, his gaze intense, and gestured silently for Giric and Auld Gommy to cross.

Pudge cursed about things not going to plan but sent the second pair across. Kester pointed them toward where Weesil was hiding, then waved to Mook and Robena.

"Ye ready, Robbie? Keep yer feet up, and ye'll no' have to spend the day in wet boots," the giant advised quietly as they urged their horses into the torrent, secure in the knowledge that Pudge was watching for trouble behind, and the rest of the band were ahead of them.

For Robena, 'twas surprisingly terrifying.

With each step, the horse plunged deeper into the river, the water closing over its knees, then up to its hips. She couldn't keep her boots out of the water—she couldn't keep her *thighs* out of the water. Mayhap 'twas because she was so much smaller than the men…whatever the reason, the rushing water pushed and tugged at her legs and kilt, threatening to tear her from her horse.

She had to just trust in the animal and keep faith in Kester.

Across the torrent, she locked eyes with him. His mouth was moving, but if he *was* saying something, she couldn't hear him over the roar of the river. Ahead of her, Mook showed no signs of trouble, and she tried to emulate his ease as she kept her focus on the man she loved, and safety.

Aye, she could do this.

The water reached above her horse's shoulders, and the animal made a nervous sound and stepped sideways. Unable to help him, she just tightened her hands on the reins and prayed she wasn't making this worse.

The water from upstream was slamming into her right hip now, crashing over the saddle as she fought to stay seated. Her kilt was soaked, her shirt was soaked, her—

A sudden, terrible thought had her twisting in the saddle. Her lute! Her *pipes.*

Last night she'd played for the men.

And she hadn't wrapped the pipes as tightly as they'd been for the first part of the journey.

The current tugged at her bundles and she lunged for the

one she knew held her pipes, desperate to reach them, to lift them out of the water's possible reach.

But the movement confused her horse, who stepped sideways again...and stumbled.

The sudden jolt sent her tumbling off the saddle and into the raging current.

The water was freezing; much colder than it had any right to be. It closed over her head, and Robena flailed her hands frantically, trying to reach the surface once more.

Her foot slammed into something—the riverbed! 'Twas not that deep!-and she thrust herself upward. As her head and shoulders emerged, she sucked in a grateful breath of air and twisted to see Kester racing along the riverbank, keeping pace with her, then pulling ahead. He shouldn't be able to outrun a river, especially not one moving this fast, but Robena saw only determination—and fear—in his expression.

Or mayhap 'twas just the cold which was slowing down her thoughts. St. Kelsi knew that each breath, each movement, of hers was becoming more sluggish. Why couldn't she seem to make her arms and legs work? She *knew* the river was shallow enough to ford, so why couldn't she just stand against the current and walk to shore?

Why was she being swept along helpless, barely able to keep her head above water?

Ahead, Kester had reached a bend and plunged into the water. He was half-swimming, half-slogging toward her. She went under, but fought her way to the surface again, choking on a mouthful of frigid water, waving one arm as best she could.

He was still coming, her savior. And he was yelling something—she had no idea what.

Yelling, and pointing.

Half-submerged, Robena twisted to look upstream...and wished she hadn't.

A heavy branch—almost a tree in its own right—slammed into her shoulder. She tried to grab onto it, but 'twas larger than her, and pushed her under.

Everything was dimmer beneath the water, the rocks under her and the branch above her, each pulling her in a different direction. Her shoulder ached, her lungs burned.

Then something knocked against her back, forcing the air from her lungs….

And everything went black.

CHAPTER 8

KESTER'S HEART—AND stomach, and veins, and very soul—were frozen, and it had nothing to do with the temperature of the water. 'Twas fear. He couldn't recall ever being so afraid, and it had nothing to do with himself and everything to do with the woman in his arms.

He'd watched Robena fall off her horse into the rushing water, and his body had acted without any sort of prompt from his mind. One moment he was crouching there, silently urging her across the river, and the next he was running. He'd managed to get ahead of her and plunge into the water, right around the time that branch had pulled her under.

Luckily, the water was shallow, and he'd had little trouble standing fast against the torrent and pulling her from beneath the surface.

But now…now she was draped across his lap and his horse was galloping toward safety…and she still wasn't moving.

He glanced down at the sodden woman and breathed another prayer. "Just a wee bit longer, lass," he murmured. "Ye'll be warm soon."

"Is he breathing?" called Weesil from behind him.

By the time Kester had exited the water, a dripping Robena in his arms, his men had joined him, leading his horse. He wasn't sure how and when Pudge had crossed the river, but he was thundering along behind them now as well.

Kester's arm tightened around her shoulders and he leaned forward, urging his horse faster.

"She's breathing," he heard Pudge growl. "She'll live."

The older man sounded as worried as Kester felt.

"Dear Heavenly Father! Look at his face!"

At Auld Gommy's screech, Kester instinctively glanced at Robena. Her head was tipped back over his arm, her pale face pointed at the cloudless sky. Her eyes were closed, her breathing shallow, and her skin far too pale.

"*His mustache!*" Giric gasped. "Robbie's lost his mustache!"

From the corner of his eye, Kester saw Auld Gommy cross himself. "Sweet Christ Almighty," the old man prayed, "the current was strong enough to rip the lad's mustache clear off his face!"

"He's a she, ye dumb shite," Pudge called out.

Behind them, Mook rumbled, "Who's a she?"

"*He!*"

"He's a she?" he repeated. "Which he? Me he? Is me a she?"

"*Jesu Christo*, ye're an idiot," muttered Pudge. "*Robbie's* a she. Look at her! Look at the laird!"

Giric clucked his tongue. "Och, Pudge is right. The MacBain wouldnae hold a lad so close. Robbie's a *lass?*"

"She's the Oliphant lass he fell in love with," Pudge explained.

Kester set his jaw, pulling Robena closer. Aye, he'd fallen in love with her. He *loved* her, and look what his stupidity had done to her.

"Where are we going?" Auld Gommy called out. "No' that I'm complaining, if ye think galloping willy-nilly westward will help the lass. But if ye want some nourishing broth, I'm going to need a fire."

"There's a village ahead, mayhap two miles," Pudge explained.

Kester wasn't certain who 'twas who asked, "Which one?" but before he could answer, Pudge did it for him.

"'Tis on Murray land. A Murray village, but they dinnae ken us as enemies on this side of the land, so we should be able to find shelter."

"*Which* Murray village, is what I'm asking." That was definitely Weesil.

"I cannae tell ye the name," growled Pudge. "Because then ye'll look at a map and be able to tell exactly where we are. Surely ye've noticed, thus far in the narrative, we've been sufficiently vague about where exactly in the Highlands we actually are? Naming the town will make it too obvious. 'Tis also possible the narrator is making shite up and doesnae actually have any real understanding of basic Scottish geography, but far be it from me to disparage such an intelligent and graceful narrator."

The men were silent for a few moments, the only sounds the pounding of their horse's hooves as they thundered westward. Finally, Weesil said, "Aye, fair enough."

Then, in the distance, he saw smoke from a hearth, and he dug his heels into his horse's side, ignoring his men.

Thank *fook* this village had a tavern. As he threw himself from the saddle, clutching Robena to him, Kester found himself praying there were rooms upstairs for rent. He left his men to care for his exhausted horse and strode inside.

Cradling the woman he loved, he planted his boots and glared at the man who'd frozen in the middle of stirring something thick and bubbling over the fire.

"A room, *now!*" he demanded. "A fire, and a big bowl of

whatever that is!" Once Robena woke—and she *would* wake—she'd be hungry, for certes.

The Murray man just gaped at him.

Did he recognize Kester? He recognized the MacBain plaid, undoubtedly, but would that be trouble? It didn't matter; Kester would gladly forfeit his freedom—his very life—to keep Robena safe.

Slowly, the man straightened, wiping his hands on his apron. "Aye, milord, but—"

"*Now!*" repeated Kester, hefting Robena so her head lolled against his shoulder.

"But this is soap, milord."

A cautious sniff confirmed that, aye, there were more florals and less meat in the pot than necessary for a stew.

"Then a bowl of something *edible*," he snapped. "The fire is more important."

As Kester took the stairs two at a time behind the proprietor, Robena began to shiver. That was a good sign, aye? That she was waking? For certes, as the Murray man began to build up the fire in the small room, Kester was gratified to see her open her eyes, her gaze dazed, as she tried to determine where she was.

"Shh, lass," he whispered against her hair, trying to take her shivering into his own body and grant her some warmth. "'Twill be aright."

But would it?

Aye, she was alive, but he'd come *so close* to losing her. Now that she was safe, Kester's body was reacting to what *might've* happened.

He was barely aware of the proprietor's words as the man bowed his way out the door, knowing Pudge or Giric would pay the man whatever he asked, since the proprietor didn't realize the MacBains had originally come to Murray land to cause mischief.

Now, Robena was all that mattered.

Whispering nonsensical promises and cursing his heavy hands, Kester stripped Robena's plaid from her waist and pulled her soaked shirt over her head. He had no time to hang them properly, and instead turned his attention to the bindings around her breasts.

She was unable to help, standing there before the hearth, clinging to him, shivering so hard he thought she might fall over. She gave no indication she saw him or understood what had happened, and each moment that passed without her being warm seemed a lifetime.

Finally, in frustration, Kester pulled his dagger from his side and sliced through the wrappings, leaving them to fall to the floor as he scooped her up.

Tucking her into bed was difficult because she couldn't seem to release him. And, truth be told, he didn't want to let her go either.

Ever.

"Hold a moment, Robena," he whispered gruffly, knowing where he belonged.

Sure enough, as soon as he stripped out of his sword belt, boots, and shirt and climbed into the bed with her, she latched onto him as if her life depended on it.

Mayhap it did.

He wrapped himself around her, and slowly her shivers subsided. Thank *fook* 'twas summertime, even if late in the season, and the water hadn't been truly frigid. But 'twas only his stupidity in allowing his men—and himself—one last adventure, which had resulted in Robena's current state.

"I'm sorry, lass. Ye'll never ken how sorry. I should never have agreed to this."

"Dinnae blame yerself."

Her voice startled him enough to pull back and peer down into her eyes. Her half-grin was wry, and she pressed her cold palms to his back, as if encouraging him to return to her.

"Kester, I wanted to come along as much as the rest of yer men. I was just stupid enough to risk my life for my pipes—" She stiffened with a gasp. "My pipes?"

He shushed her, running his hands along whatever skin he could reach, trying to give her all of his warmth. "Yer horse was frightened but made it across. With all its bundles, as near as we can tell. I'll check on them for ye."

"Thank—" A yawn interrupted her. "Thank ye. I dinnae ken why I'm so—" Another yawn.

He tucked her head under his chin and stretched one heavy thigh over her legs, ignoring how perfect she felt in his arms.

"Ye've had a battle, lass, and 'tis nae wonder ye're tired. That blow to yer head alone was scary—"

"I'm fine, Kester. The branch didnae hit me, just pulled me under. I likely swallowed half the river."

Saints above, the reminder was as chilling as her hands. Unable to help himself, he examined her head with his fingers until he was satisfied in her claim; there was no lump, no blood.

Still, a near-drowning and catatonic shock from the cold was nothing to sneeze at.

As if on cue, Robena let out a mighty sneeze then sniffled and apologized.

Smiling, he kissed the top of her head. "Rest, love. I'll be here."

Forever.

After a while, her breathing evened in sleep and Kester decided she was sufficiently warm. And *because* she was sufficiently warm, his body was having a hard time remembering she'd had a near-death experience today.

Hypothermia apparently meant little to his cock, which kept insistently trying to poke her thigh.

Cursing himself, he slid from the bed then gently draped another blanket atop her mound of blankets, hoping 'twould be enough to replace his body heat.

He took his time hanging her clothes to dry and pulling his boots back on, and finally decided he'd dallied long enough. Best get on with seeing how his future looked.

Downstairs, he found his men sitting solemnly around a table, enjoying *actual* stew. The innkeeper bustled up with a bowl for him, which Kester sniffed suspiciously before deciding it smelled a little like soap, and hazarded a bite.

He couldn't taste it, nor the ale the proprietor served them all. Kester ate, but the food was heavy in his stomach.

All he could think of was the woman upstairs, and how close he'd come to losing her.

Weesil assured him Robena's pipes were unharmed—they were barely wet—and he'd taken the liberty of arranging everything in her bundles to dry. Including, he admitted without meeting Kester's eyes, a fine yellow silk gown and chemise.

"So, she *is* a lass?" Mook muttered in confusion to Giric.

The handsome man was flushing in embarrassment, which Kester might've found amusing had he been in a different state of mind.

"Aye, Mook," mumbled Giric. "And we've spent the journey talking of our penises."

"She sang a song about pissing on Auld Gommy! Lasses dinnae stand against bushes when they piss!"

Giric sighed and patted the big man's arm. "Aye. 'Tis disconcerting."

That wasn't the word for it.

After a subdued meal, Kester stood once more. Let his men drink themselves to sleep tonight if they'd be sleeping in the stables. *He* planned to spend the evening holding Robena and trying to feed her warm food.

Pudge stopped him before he could climb the stairs, holding out a packet Kester recognized.

"Gordon's missive?" Kester opened the oiled leather envelope. "It appears dry."

The older warrior nodded. "I thought it didnae need to spend the night in yer saddlebags, where any thief might wander by."

Kester mutely nodded—in agreement, or thanks, he wasn't certain—and swallowed the lump in his throat. This bloody missive wasn't the cause of his current predicament, but 'twas the excuse the King had needed to get him to the Games and married to Murray's daughter.

"Will…she be aright?" Pudge hazarded.

Sighing, Kester ran his free hand through his hair. "Aye. She's sleeping now and is warm enough. I…." He shook his head then swallowed, unsure how to express his terror. "When she went under, Pudge…."

The older man nodded. "Ye didnae hesitate to save her. Ye love her."

He tried to whisper *"Aye,"* even though it hadn't been a question. He cleared his throat and tried again. "She cannae swim."

His friend heard the words he didn't say. Pudge clasped him on the shoulder. "I'm sorry it has to be like this, Laird."

Kester's fingers curled into a fist, not caring that he crumbled Gordon's missive.

Nay.

He was done sacrificing himself and his future for the King. Aye, aligning with Murray would end the feud and bring his clan peace…but aligning with the Oliphants could bring them prosperity—and his heart's desire.

He and Robena were meant to be together.

Nay, he could not accept that there was no hope for a

future between them. Not with how much he loved her. Not with how he felt today when he thought he'd lost her.

"Nay," he repeated, his gaze hardening as he began to climb. "It does *no'* have to be this way."

And he thought he might've heard from behind him a very faint, "Good luck, Laird."

When he entered her room, Kester found Robena as he'd left her, a bowl of stew steaming beside her bed.

He stripped down and gathered her in his arms once more. She roused enough to eat a few mouthfuls, although he could tell she wasn't really awake. Thank the saints this seemed like a normal sleep, born of exhaustion and bone-deep cold, rather than the unnatural sleep of a few hours ago.

Now she slept peacefully, the faintest smudge of stew on her lower lip. Gently, he used the pad of one thumb to wipe it away, and his touch lingered on her lips.

"I love ye, lass."

When he slid one arm under her, she turned to him so trustingly, as if she had no cares in the world, and they were not lying naked in bed together.

For warmth.

He almost believed the lie.

"I love ye," he whispered again. "And I thought I'd lost ye."

In that moment when she went under, his heart had died. And when he'd pulled her from the water and felt her heart beating against his palm, even as she coughed up water—and then her lunch....

Kester shuddered and pressed a kiss to her temple. "I love ye, Robena Oliphant, and I cannae lose ye again." A yawn interrupted him. "I *will no'* lose ye again."

On that whispered vow, he hauled her up against him, and his eyes fluttered closed.

Mᴍᴍ. Robena was warm. Deliciously warm. And cozy, too.

She was lying on her side, her hand pillowing her cheek, and as she slowly woke, she couldn't help the contented little wriggle her rear end made, delighting in the all-encompassing *warmth* after the frigid fright she'd had earlier.

That little wriggle was interrupted, however, by something hard.

Something hard pressed against—she experimentally uncurled a bit, arching her back—against *all* of her. Something hard, something warm, curled around her, protecting her.

She grinned into the semi-darkness.

There was a hand on her hip, and that's when she realized she was very, very naked.

Well, that's the perfect state to be when this particular hardness is pressed against ye, aye?

Aye.

Yesterday, she'd almost died. Oh, she'd told Kester it had been more fear than injury which had put her to sleep as he'd pulled her from the water, but the ice cold hadn't helped either.

But he'd cared for her. He *cared* for her.

Even now, he was protecting her, warming her. Her belly was full, and she was warm and cherished.

He mumbled something in his sleep, his breath warm against the back of her neck, and his arm slid around her. The movement snugged her arse up against the most intriguing bit of *hardness*, and his hand came to rest *almost* touching her breast.

Well, almost *isnae good enough, is it?*

Because after yesterday, after the last days of being *almost* with Kester, Robena knew what she wanted.

'Twas time to make him hers.

Or make her his.

She was unclear on the terminology.

Sex. Ye want to have sex with him.

Aye, that was it.

Still smiling, she began, very slowly, to scooch down the bed, while gently lifting the heavy forearm which lay across her torso. It wasn't easy, and it resulted in him shifting once or twice, but finally...

Finally...

She was able to rest his hand down, once more.

Where it belonged.

And when his callused palm cupped her small breast, almost completely covering it, she couldn't swallow down the delighted moan, even knowing *she'd* been the one to place him there.

'Twas amazing how *wonderful* this man could make her feel, even without meaning to. His fingers tightened, and although it had most certainly been involuntary, she gasped and surged backward, her arse cradling his cock, flexing against it.

'Twas his turn to make a noise very like a groan, as his thumb and forefinger found her nipple and rolled it.

This time she didn't bother trying to swallow down her response, but arched in his hold, her hand reaching behind to his hip, and squeezing. St. Kelsi help her, if he wasn't awake soon, she had to ensure he would be....

His movements languid and gentle, Kester's callused fingers caressed the sensitive skin around her nipple, driving her mad. His thumb brushed against the swollen bud and the sensation shot straight down to the junction of her thighs, where her hips jerked as if he'd caressed *another* swollen bud.

Instinctively, her hand dropped from his hips to her curls, searching for release. She involuntarily pressed her arse back once more, and *this* time, his cock was erect enough to slide below the globes of her cheeks...between her legs.

She heard him suck in a breath on a hiss as her wetness

coated him. His cock rested against the opening of her core, but from *behind*. 'Twas deliciously wicked, and she could feel herself pulsing around his hardness, aching for him.

Aching to be filled.

His hand fell away from her breast, gliding along her stomach until his fingers cupped hers, which were circling her clitoris. His fingertips nudged hers out of the way, and that's when she decided he was most definitely awake.

But the silence of the room, lit only by the gentle glow from the hearth coals—the remains of the fire he'd lit to care for her—seemed too sacred to break with words. So instead of encouraging him, she reached again for his hip, pulling him closer, allowing the whole of her back to rest against his chest.

'Twas an intimate position, one which she wouldn't have considered. Dimly, she wondered if Wynda's book, as dictated by the Gray Lady, included this position.

Nay, because his cock isnae actually in ye yet.

But she could imagine how it *could* be. And if he continued to caress her core this way, she would demand it.

His fingers teased her gently, the way he had during their nights in the woods together. He knew exactly how to caress her pearl, the center of her pleasure, then drag his forefinger along her swollen slit. Her lips were wet with need for him, and as he pressed one finger ever so minutely into her, she couldn't contain the moan which escaped her lips.

She pressed back again, trying to give him more room to slide further into her, but he refrained. "Kester," she whimpered, finally breaking her vow. "*Please.*"

He hummed, his mouth near enough to her ear she could feel his breath. "Lass, ye were half-dead from cold a few hours ago."

"I'm hot now." 'Twas stupid, but her brain couldn't come up with anything better to announce. "*So* hot."

His chuckle was dry. "Aye," he agreed, languidly dragging

his finger through her slit once more, even as he flexed his hips. "Ye are."

She'd gasped at his movement, deciding she liked his *cock* sliding across her core even better than his fingers. "Do that again!"

"What, this?" He chuckled again as he flexed, pressing his cock forward briefly.

The motion was delightfully maddening; the tip of his cock brushed against her clitoris before withdrawing.

Deciding to take matters into her own hands, Robena tightened her hold on his hip, fingers digging into his skin, and flexed her own hips. With him remaining still, she was able to slide *herself* along his cock and choose the best angle, as well.

She was riding him while lying on her side.

Each buck of her hips drew him closer and drew *her* closer to her pleasure. She bit her bottom lip, trying to contain the sounds of pleasure sure to be wrung from her.

He was breathing hard, and unless she was mistaken, he seemed to be having trouble containing—

"Lass," he rasped. "Ye're killing me."

Pleasure built inside her, but also frustration. This felt divine, but not quite what she needed. "Show me!" Her gasp was half a moan. "Please, Kester!"

His groan of surrender matched hers, and then his arm was beneath her, lifting her.

Not far, though; she found herself in the same position, lying with her back to his chest, her head resting on his shoulder. Only now his hard thighs rested between hers—her own thighs spread over them, spreading *her* to his touch.

And he touched her—aye, he touched her. With both hands available now, one of them cupped her breast, rolling the nipple, while the other delved into her curls.

And his cock slid along her wet core.

Unable to help herself, she reached between her legs and pressed her fingertips against the hardness bringing her such pleasure, squeezing it closer to her. It still wasn't close enough, no matter how hard he thrust.

She needed him inside her.

With a burst of strength, she sat straight upward, wrenching a gasp from him. The motion cradled his cock between her thighs, and she reached for his legs. All she'd have to do was slide him inside of her….

Would that work?

"Can we have sex like this?"

His hands were on her hips and he made a noise halfway between a laugh and a groan. "Ye're a virgin, lass."

She twisted so she could frown over her shoulder at him. "What does that have aught to do with the question?"

"Yer first time should be…special." His voice sounded hoarse, but in the dim light, 'twas hard to see his expression.

She was feeling strangely irritated now, and she wasn't certain if 'twas because her orgasm had been delayed, or because he wasn't wholeheartedly taking her virginity. Robena huffed as she threw her leg over one of his hips.

He tried to help her slide off him, but that wasn't what she wanted. Instead, she twisted around until she was facing him fully, then lifted one of her legs back over him.

Now she straddled his hips once more, but facing him.

"I *ken* we can have sex like this." She'd seen the illustrations in Wynda's book.

His hands had landed on her hips once more and now slid up her sides. "Are ye certain, lass?" He sounded strained.

"Aye, Kester." She leaned forward—the movement pressing his cock between her curls and his stomach—and said in a wickedly teasing tone, "I want ye to *fook* me, milord. I want to feel yer cock deep in me as I find pleasure. I want to scream yer name."

"*Jesu Christo,*" he breathed, already reaching for her breasts. Then he repeated, "*Jesu Christo,* Robena. I almost lost ye."

"Aye, but ye saved me. And we might no' have forever—" Her voice caught, refusing to allow herself to focus on that right now. "But we have tonight."

His hands stilled, and she watched *something* contort his expression.

In a blink of an eye, he went from shocked to determined, and he lifted his palms to cup her cheeks. This required her to lean forward, toward him, and since that meant his cock jutted hard against her clitoris, she didn't mind at all.

"Lass…Robena, is *now* an appropriate time to tell ye I love ye?"

His voice sounded half-tortured, half-exasperated, and she allowed her fond smile to bloom. "What are we now? Sixty-five percent of the way through our story?" She pretended to think about it as she teased him, her hands supporting herself on his shoulders. "Aye, I think 'tis appropriate."

"Well…." His lips curled in a smile as he tugged her closer. "We might be at sixty-eight percent by now."

"Just say it, Kester."

"I love ye, Robena Oliphant."

A sense of *rightness* melted through her, and she sighed softly as she lowered her lips to his. "And I love ye," she whispered against his skin.

With a groan, he slid his palm around to the back of her head, pulling her closer for a kiss. She cupped his cheeks—delightfully scratchy with the days' worth of whiskers—in her hands and held him.

This position shifted her forward, until the tip of his cock pressed against her entrance. 'Twas completely natural to sink back, to seat herself atop it. They both stiffened at the sensation, then slowly relaxed, their lips still pressed to one another.

They were sharing the same air.

Robena had never felt so *full*. Full, but also…whole. As if a part of her had been missing all this time and *he'd* been the one to complete her.

She wanted to move, but he was still lying still beneath her.

So, she flexed her hips just slightly, remembering the way she'd moved when she'd been on her side. The motion wrenched a groan from him, but she was too busy gasping in delight, as a million tiny points of pleasure burst inside her.

"Lass," he growled, sounding in pain, "are ye—? Do ye need…?"

"I need to move." She planted her palms on either side of his head. "I need—"

She wasn't certain what she needed.

But he was.

His hands on her hips once more, Kester showed her how to rest her weight on her knees, so he could slide in and out of her from beneath. At first, his movements were slow and subtle, allowing her time to get used to the sensation.

But soon, she was panting, her eyes squeezed shut, her entire being focused on her core and where they became one. Once, she'd thought such sensations overwhelming…but now, she didn't understand how she'd lived without this.

"Oh, St. Kelsi protect me!" she gasped, as she inched closer to her release. "Kester, *please*."

As he thrust into her, he commanded, "Look at me, Robena."

How could she disobey such an order? She met his blue eyes, which were bright in the dim light.

"I love ye, Robena," he growled, each beat punctuated with a thrust. "I dinnae care what the King says; ye're mine and I'm yers."

Oh, St. Kelsi's vocal cords! She was *so close*.

All she could do was pant in agreement, hoping he'd understand.

"Robena, whatever the future holds, we'll face it together."

What was he saying? Was he saying what she *thought* he was saying?

"I love ye, lass."

And that was all she needed.

Her pleasure burst over her, white-hot and desperate, pulsing around him as she shot straight into the air.

She screamed his name, hitting a note she'd never thought to try for before.

Apparently, her pleasure triggered his own, because he groaned long and low, and dimly she was aware of a flood of warmth against her womb... But each pulse milked him further and harder until she was panting with exhaustion.

St. Kelsi help her, she'd never experienced anything as wonderful as *that*.

Sated now, Robena collapsed forward, her cheek landing against his shoulder. She listened to his heart beating under her ear, listened to the glorious sound of his breathing slowing to match hers.

They were still joined.

She smiled, and one of her palms came to rest against the side of his neck.

"I love ye," she murmured. "*Always*, Kester."

His arms tightened around her. "And I love ye." His voice was a quiet murmur, one she felt as much as heard. "No' just here and now, lass, but forever."

She closed her eyes on his vow, a smile on her lips.

CHAPTER 9

MOOK WAS STILL SNORING, stretched out on the floor of the main room when Kester crept downstairs the morning after he'd made Robena his. After he'd almost lost her. After she'd changed his world.

I love ye. Always, Kester.

Aye, his stomach was tight with worry, but those words… they made him hopeful for the future, for the first time since he'd met Robena. For the first time since Laird Murray's plan had been announced. For the first time since the MacBains had lost Kester's Meadow.

He wasn't certain what the future would hold, but he knew she'd be in it.

"Wake up, ye lazy shite." He nudged Mook in the side, which did nothing except bruise his toe.

As he was limping toward one of the stools, Giric rolled off the bench along the wall. "Wazzat?" the handsome man muttered, sitting on his arse on the floor. "Time to go already?"

"Ye lads had some fun last night, eh?" Kester gestured to

the proprietor to bring him some ale and brown bread with butter. "I thought ye were supposed to sleep in the stables."

Giric yawned as he clamored to his feet and joined his laird. "Pudge and Weesil did that. Auld Gommy disappeared with one of the serving wenches." Giric winced and covered his eyes with one palm "Nay, I dinnae want to speculate, *thankyeverramuch.*"

Ah. 'Twas becoming clear that Giric—rejected in favor of the eldest MacBain warrior—had consoled himself with drink.

"So I should no' order oysters in cream sauce, and pickled vegetables with mutton to break my fast?"

Giric turned green. "If ye do, I'll vomit on yer boots."

Kester made a show of examining his feet. "I like these boots, so mayhap I'll just stick with brown bread." He nodded his thanks to the proprietor and gestured for him to bring more.

Giric was picking at his bread as Pudge and Weesil entered and Mook slowly woke. Soon, all of them—save Auld Gommy, and Kester was also happy not to speculate—were gathered around the table.

He sat with his back to the wall so he could keep an eye on the stairs. And when Robena finally descended, he was the first to see her. Sucking in a breath, he slowly stood.

God's Wounds, she was lovely. She'd worn that yellow silk for her sister's wedding, which meant she'd been wearing it during his "tour" of the secret passages, and their kisses. Mayhap 'twas because he'd broken her heart that day—whatever that meant—but he hadn't noticed how *lovely* she looked in it.

Or mayhap 'twas because today she wore her hair down around her shoulders, clean and curly from its accidental washing yesterday.

Or mayhap 'twas the shy, secret smile she sent his way, the

gentle coloring of her cheeks, and the reminder of what she'd screamed last night with her legs wrapped around his waist.

He was grinning proudly as he crossed to take her hand.

"Holy shite," murmured Giric, wide-eyed. "Robbie *is* a lass!"

'Twas Weesil who stood stiffly and bowed, his fist over his heart. One by one, the men followed, as Robena blushed.

"What happened to her mustache?" Mook whispered loudly.

Giric, who was sitting once more with his forehead planted in his palm, groaned. "There *was* nae mustache. 'Twas fake. For shite's sake, I cannae believe I didnae see it!"

Kester couldn't help feeling a little smug at that.

"I'll take it as a compliment, Giric," Robena said softly, "that I could fool *ye*."

He groaned again. "I cannae believe we joked about…*every-thing*. Pissing. Pleasuring women. *Our favorite part*."

This time, Robena was grinning as she met Kester's eyes. "I'm still me. Ye can still joke with me."

"Nay, ye're no'." Giric still hadn't looked up. "Ye have *tits*."

'Twas one thing to listen to his Robena joke with another man, and another thing altogether to hear that man—and a handsome one at that—admire her tits. Kester growled.

Giggling, Robena pressed against his arm, so he could feel those same tits under her gown.

The sensation—the knowledge she couldn't bind them because he'd cut her wrappings—and the memory of how they'd tasted in his mouth last night, made his cock stir happily.

He cleared his throat.

"Lads, we'll be at the Games in two days if we ride hard. Once there, I'll meet with Murray." He glanced down at Robena, who was chewing on her lower lip as she stared up at him. Taking a deep breath, he continued. "And I'll tell him there'll be nae alliance."

The responses from his men were varied, but Robena's was all that mattered. Something like hope had flickered in her eyes at the announcement, but it faded to worry. "The King…."

He didn't allow her to finish. With a sharp shake of his head, he faced his men. "I will no' marry Murray's daughter." He kept his voice pitched low in case the proprietor was listening. "I'll face the King's wrath if it comes to that. Pudge will take my place as laird if I have to—"

She tugged hard on his hand with both of hers. When he glanced down at her once more, 'twas to see her frowning fiercely.

"I love ye, Kester MacBain, but I dinnae want ye hurt just so we can be together."

A reluctant smile tugged at his lips and he bent to press a quick kiss to her lips. "I love ye too, Robena. Hopefully, it willnae come to that."

"Fook me," rumbled Mook. "Robbie *is* a lass, and the MacBain loves her?"

Robena's grin was rueful as she shook her head, likely at the big man's inability to accept her transformation. "I'll go get changed once more."

"Why?" Kester's fingers tightened on hers to let her know she had his support.

With a sigh, she hiked up her skirts and turned for the stairs. "I dinnae mind feeling pretty, but a kilt will be easier to wear if we're riding hard."

Riding hard. The phrase reminded him of what they'd done last night and how she was likely sore this morning.

So, when they set out on their horses—after she repacked her pipes and carefully rolled gown—he made certain the pair of them rode at the rear, as was his preference.

And as the men's animals settled into their steady traveling pace, he nudged his horse next to hers. Without breaking stride, he pulled her from her saddle, and before she could do more than gasp, he'd settled her in his lap.

Like yesterday, she rode sideways, one arm supporting her back, and her thighs draped across his. Only now, she was upright, and her pert little bottom was warm as it cradled his cock.

Mayhap she understood that, because she gave him the naughtiest grin as she snaked her arms around his waist and pressed her cheek to his chest.

That night, despite her obvious exhaustion, Robena smiled as she collected their blankets. She took his hand and led him out of the circle of the firelight, and they both pretended not to hear the jibes and hoots the men called after them.

Apparently Giric had overcome his embarrassment.

Kester had never spent a day riding while holding a woman in his lap. He supposed his thighs and back might ache…but when she turned to him and gave him that devastating come-hither smile, he had no choice but to, well, come hither.

She led him into a tree.

Then another tree.

By the time she smacked into the third tree, he took the lead, finding a protected pile of pine needles out of the wind. He made quick work of laying out their blankets, and by the time he turned, she already had her boots off.

There were benefits to loving a woman who wore a kilt.

Easy access, and all that.

After, Kester wrapped them both in his plaid and settled against the bed he'd made. She was tucked up against his chest, and he smiled to feel the way their hearts beat in unison.

One of her fingers was drawing small circles on the skin of his neck, and he never wanted her to stop.

"Kester?" she whispered.

He hummed in response.

"I'm scared."

His arms tightened, knowing only that he had to protect her. But he also understood. "About tomorrow? The piping competition won't start until after sundown."

She was silent for a moment, and then he felt her shoulders shake with a sudden burst of laughter. "Can ye believe I'd forgotten about the piping competition?" She sounded disgusted with herself. "Nay, I meant…Murray."

Ah. "I'll no' let him hurt ye."

She flicked him. "'Tis no' *me* I'm scared for, ye stubborn man. I'm scared for *ye*. And what the King will do when he finds out ye're no' marrying Murray's daughter."

"I cannae marry Murray's daughter," Kester said lightly, flippantly, ignoring the worry in his own stomach, "if I'm marrying *ye*."

She blew out a breath, and her hand cupped his neck. "I love ye, Kester. But I'd rather ye be alive and someone else's than mine and—"

Her voice broke at the end, and he heard her swallow thickly.

His lips dropped to her hair.

How could one woman shoulder so much burden? "Trust me, Robena. I'll find a way for us to be together. I love ye."

She was silent for a long while. When she did speak, she sounded close to sleep. "I used to envy Lady Elspeth, ye ken. I picture her as beautiful and talented and graceful."

He snorted softly. "Mayhap. But there's nae way she's as beautiful and talented as *ye* are."

She yawned. "I notice ye didnae say *graceful*."

"Ye're wearing pine sap in yer hair from all the trees ye bumped into."

"I didnae bump into them." She couldn't manage to sound indignant. "They jumped out of naewhere and attacked me. The sap is a valiant scar from my battles."

He chuckled and kissed her again. "Go to sleep, love."

"I dinnae envy her any longer," she confessed, before another yawn overtook her.

"Really?" He knew nothing of Murray's family, much less the laird's eldest daughter. "Why?"

"Because she might be beautiful and talented and everything ye'd like in a wife…but ye're *mine*."

And long after she fell asleep, Kester MacBain smiled.

Aye, he *was* hers, and she was his. And no matter what happened tomorrow, that would be true.

God willing.

THE GAMES WERE NEARING their end as their little party arrived late the next day. Already, some of the clans who had the farthest to travel had departed, not caring about the musical competitions to come. Kester could see the empty places in the field where the grass had been trampled and broken by the camps.

Robena sat on her own horse, her shoulders straight, her expression carefully neutral as she surveyed the field.

"See the Sutherland banner, milady?" Auld Gommy was pointing solicitously. "They're the bastards to beat, excuse my language."

"How do ye ken?"

The old man scoffed. "They *always* kick everyone's arses, excuse my language. There's so damn many of them! Excuse my language."

Robena's lips twitched. "Ye dinnae have to keep excusing yer language. I've heard ye say much worse."

"Aye, and I'm hoping ye'll forget about that, afore my laird beats me black and blue for it."

She lifted her fingertips to her lips in a familiar gesture, as if trying to press her mustache back. Fortunately, since it had been swept away, she'd made no effort to create another one. On the one hand, he didn't have to taste a fooking mustache every time he wanted to kiss the woman he loved….

On the other hand, between her bare upper lip, and lack of binding around her breasts, Kester didnae think anyone would confuse her for a lad.

"There's the Murray tents!" Mook called and pointed happily.

Kester and Pudge exchanged a glance, their eyes hard.

Aye, Ian Murray had set up his camp on the cliff over-looking the loch. It meant he and his men had farther to go to reach the competition fields, but he also had the prime position from which to look over the gathered clans. Slightly above everyone, off to the west, he'd be able to look across the Games and tell himself he was more important than the others, because he had the ear of the King.

Self-important arsehole.

"Auld Gommy, ye and Weesil set up camp on the outskirts, aye? Mook, ye and Giric are in charge of scouting. Spread out and see what ye can learn. Pudge, ye come with me."

Robena clucked at her horse to move up beside his. "With *us*."

"Ye should rest for a bit, love. We had to ride hard to get here by this evening." And a hard ride last night, too. He fought the urge to reach for her, to brush his hand against hers, to remind her she belonged to him. "And I have to find the steward to deliver the Gordon's missive."

The way she cocked her brow at him said she didn't believe his excuses. "And after that ye will go to Laird Murray, aye? I will be there with ye."

He watched her for a moment before inclining his head, conceding the point. In all honesty, he wanted her at his side when he told the old bastard the MacBain wanted no alliance.

The steward was easy enough to find, and 'twas anticlimactic to turn over the oiled envelope of vellum and scrolls, knowing that missive was the excuse the King had needed to send Kester across the Highlands.

Now, they sent their horses with Weesil and set off on foot. Pudge trailed behind, but it felt natural to stroll through the encampments with Robena's hand tucked in his.

"Ye're getting looks," murmured Pudge from behind.

Kester glanced around and realized his old friend was right.

"'Tis because they think me a lad."

He snorted at her claim. "Ye're too pretty to be a lad."

"And *ye're* half-blind, if ye think me pretty."

Frowning now, he pulled her to a halt. "Dinnae say such things. Ye *are* too pretty to be a lad."

She responded with a snort of her own and pulled her hand from his to rest on her hip. Her curved, sensual, *feminine* hip. "Ye're just saying that because we've—*ahem.*"

"Aye, we've *ahemed,* and that means I can see ye for who ye really are, Robena!"

Her brow quirked, as if he'd proved her point. "And I havenae *ahemed* any of these other men, so they believe me a lad in a kilt, holding hands with ye."

Arms folded across his chest, Kester turned to glare at the men who watched, some from a distance, some not bothering to hide their interest. "They *cannae* think ye a lad," he hissed.

"They do. And imagine what that's doing to the reputation of the great Kester MacBain, to be holding the hand of a lad like he's *ahemed* that lad."

Pudge made a sound which might've been a laugh, had the man ever laughed.

"Ye think such a thing matters to me? What others think?"

Her lips twitched mischievously. "Why, MacBain, are ye saying ye dinnae care about yer reputation?"

Since she was mocking him, he scowled. "I'm no' the one gallivanting around in a kilt!"

"Aye, ye are."

"Well, aye, aright, I *am* gallivanting about in a kilt. But I'm supposed to."

She leaned forward, her hands still on her hips, and gave him a saucy smile. "Well, I'm doing it for a good reason, and *I* dinnae care about my reputation."

"Ye should," he growled.

"Because ye want to marry me? Lady MacBain should be demure and no'-at-all-scandalous?"

Why in the hell were they having this debate here and now?

"Lady MacBain will be brave and talented and the winner of the Highland Piping Competition." When her expression melted, his scowl eased, and he stepped toward her and lowered his voice. "Robena, I love ye for who ye are. I just wish ye'd let these people see that, too."

She opened her mouth to reply, but they were interrupted by a loud call.

"Laird MacBain! My master commands ye to quit delaying!" They both turned to see a smug-looking man in a Murray kilt pointing up the hill toward the Murray encampment on the edge of the cliff. "He bids ye come seal yer alliance."

"I want nae alliance," Kester growled as he snagged Robena's hand in his and strode toward his enemy.

It wasn't until he noticed Robena out of breath at his side that he forced his steps to slow, so the pair of them took their time climbing up to the Murray's tent. He stood outside it, flanked by two burly warriors who scowled at Kester as if they blamed him for all of life's inconveniences.

Well, at least all of those inconveniences involving sheep dyeing, pin-stealing, and flower-picking.

Was it any wonder why Kester was grinning as he pulled Robena to a stop before Ian Murray?

"Laird Murray," he acknowledged, inclining his head. "Ye're looking as…*lairdly* as ever."

The older man—who wasn't just leaning toward fat, but falling, running, *leaping* toward fat—scowled. "And *ye're* late." He tugged at his enormous dark beard. "Ye think to insult my men by bringing only two of yers? An ancient grandda and a green lad?"

Behind Kester, Pudge growled something insulting and stepped forward, likely to prove he was as strong and capable as any man half his age, but Kester held up his hand to stop him.

With his lips still curled up at the corners, he jerked his chin. "My right-hand man, Pudge MacBain, who was the one responsible for that clever scheme involving yer chickens. And this is Robbie Oliphant, who's going to win the piping competition."

Murray did little more than glance at Pudge, but his scowl focused on the face Kester still held Robena's hand. "And ye're parading him about as yer heir, is that it? I cannae think ye're *fooking* the lad."

'Twas intended to be an insult, of course. But Kester didn't bother to hide his snort of amusement. The old bastard really thought Robena was a lad? Mayhap he *was* blind.

"See," Robena hissed merrily from the corner of her mouth, as she pulled her hand from his and giving Murray a friendly wave. "I told ye so."

As Kester shook his head, Murray waved away one of his guards, who ducked into the tent at their back. "Enough with the niceties." *Niceties?* "Ye've been a thorn in my side for years, MacBain, and although 'tis been humorous to watch ye try to keep yer tiny clan alive, wouldn't it be so much easier to just accept defeat and join the clans together under my leadership?" His tone changed to mocking. "Ye ken I've found a way to make peace between our clans. A marriage alliance, one of which the King approves, and ye'll gain the meadow ye think is yers."

Strangely, all of Kester's good humor had fled. With a growl, he stepped forward. "The meadow *is* ours, auld man, but for yer dishonorable actions. It'll always be the MacBain's bane, but we can survive without it." The way his chin jerked toward Robena was unintended, but true. "We'll ally with other clans and be strong enough to *take* back the meadow— or ignore it altogether."

"Ye dinnae need to take it back; it'll be yers again if ye marry my daughter."

With each moment that passed, Kester knew he was doing the right thing. With a curt shake of his head, he folded his arms across his chest.

"I'll no' marry yer daughter, Murray, no' even to regain that which belongs to my clan."

The older laird reared back, surprise on his face. "Ye would put yer own wants afore that of yer clan?"

"My clan needs prosperity, aye, but I'm coming to realize there are other ways of gaining it—other clans to ally with— besides pandering to yer spoiled offspring. My people will support my decision." *And I'll be able to marry the woman I love.*

"But the King—"

"The King is a good man," growled Kester, "and when I explain what ye did after my mother's death, I hope he'll understand ye're no' the aggrieved party ye've been playing."

Beneath the beard, Murray's mouth twisted in a scowl, and he opened it—

But was interrupted when the flap to the tent opened behind him and his burly warrior emerged, tugging a female. She was dressed in a cream-colored gown, her dark hair—the same shade as the Murray's—falling freely down around her shoulders. 'Twas decorated with a lopsided flower crown, and the bouquet she carried in one hand looked to have been decimated by anger or fear. Aye, she was lovely, and clearly didn't want to be here.

She also looked to be about seven years old.

"My eldest daughter, Lady Elspeth," announced Murray sullenly. "Yer bride."

At Kester's side, Robena was busy trying to swallow her laughter, and Kester felt his lips twitching once more.

Lady Elspeth Murray was a *lassie*. Barely more than a bairn. And her father wanted to marry her off to an enemy like Kester MacBain to keep the peace?

'Twas ludicrous.

Almost as ridiculous as the way the lassie wailed and threw her bouquet at her father.

"I'll *no'* marry him, Da!" she screamed, yanking her arm from her guard's hold, and stomping her foot. "Ye cannae make me!"

Her father whirled on her, one finger raised, and bellowed right back, "Ye'll do what I tell ye, ye ungrateful bairn! Ye owe it to yer clan to make peace!"

"I dinnae *care* about *peace*!" She stomped again, her face going red. "I dinnae want to *marry* him!" One skinny arm flung out, a finger pointed at Kester.

He felt the need to defend himself. "For what 'tis worth, milady, I have nae interest in marrying ye, either. My heart belongs to another."

"See, Da? I cannae marry him!"

Her father ignored both of their arguments. "Ye *will* marry the MacBain, Elspeth! As yer laird and father, I'm telling ye ye'll marry the man I choose, and nae one else."

The lassie froze, a look of fury on her face fading to one of determination.

"Fine," she snarled.

Kester suspected something amiss, and had already lowered his arms to be ready, when the girl gathered up her skirts, whirled about, and ran for the cliff.

She went over before any of them could reach for her.

Her father's bellowed, *"Elspeth!"* almost drowned out the sound of the splash, far below.

Kester was moving toward the cliff face when a blur in Oliphant plaid streaked past him. He didn't have time to react before Robena—because of course 'twas Robena—tucked her legs, straightened her arms, and dove off the cliff after the girl.

He skidded to a stop at the edge, peering incredulously at the double splashes far below.

Murray thundered to a halt beside him. "Elspeth!" he bellowed at the loch, as if that would help, his gaze frantic.

Almost as frantic as Kester's own. Why wasn't she coming up for air? Had she hurt herself?

"How deep is it down there?" he snapped at Murray.

"Deep enough," the older man snapped right back, leaning as far as he dared over the ledge. "I dinnae see them. They should've landed aright. Do ye think yer lad will be able to save her?"

"I doubt it," Kester muttered, kicking off his boots and dropping his sword belt to the ground. "She cannae swim."

As he went over the edge of the cliff, bracing himself for the splash, he heard Laird Ian Murray bellow, *"She?"*

Idiot. Robena's no' even wearing her mustache.

CHAPTER 10

As the water closed over her head, an idle thought flitted through Robena's mind.

Ye've done some dumb shite in yer life, but this is undoubtedly the dumbest.

Right.

Because she couldn't swim.

But really, how hard could it be? Mayhap she just couldn't swim because she hadn't *applied* herself well enough.

Well, if there's any time to apply yerself, 'tis now.

This conversation happened in a moment, between the first icy touch of the loch and the realization 'twas too late in the day to rely on any help from the sun, in terms of seeing farther than an arms-reach. *Shite.*

Did ye really just jump off a cliff to save a lassie, and have nae idea how to find her? Idiot.

Well, really, she just had to be logical about this. Robena had noted the location of Elspeth's splash and she knew she'd landed practically in the same place. So, unless the girl had hit the water and started swimming away, she should be right around....

Since time had apparently decided to slow down a bit, Robena used this period to kick about randomly with her boots.

Sure enough, one of her feet connected solidly with something below her, and a stream of bubbles whooshed past her, as if expelled from a mouth of a lassie who'd just been booted in the head.

Huzzah! But also, *oh dear* because it meant Elspeth now had less air than planned.

How much air does a wee girl need if she's planning on killing herself to avoid marrying Kester?

Spurred on by the chilling thought, Robena doubled over, waving her arms through the water in approximately the same place where she'd kicked Elspeth. Sure enough, her questing fingers snagged in what was either floating seaweed —*Lochweed? Is that a thing?*—or hair.

She tugged.

The angry squeal was audible even under water, and Robena knew she'd found Elspeth.

She pulled the girl toward her—hoping she wasn't pulling them both deeper—and tried to ignore Elspeth's squirming. Did the lassie *really* want to die? Was marriage to Kester such a horrible fate?

'Twas about this time—time slowing down or not—that Robena realized *her* lungs were starting to burn. *Double-shite.* As she closed the fingers of her left hand around what she hoped was the neckline of the lassie's gown, Robena tipped her chin upward.

Or in the direction she *hoped* was upward.

Was that...? Did the water become lighter up there? Sluggishly, she was able to glance below, where Elspeth fought her in the distant darkness. Aye, 'twas darker down there, which meant....

What did it mean? Why wasn't her brain working?

Air. Ye need air. Idiot.

Aye, and air was that way. Well, light was that way, so hopefully that way was *up*, and air would be up there.

Aye. Aye, that made sense.

Now, to figure out how to swim.

Well…how hard could it be? Just sort of…kick? And she had one hand free, didn't she?

Her limbs seemed to be working as slowly as her mind. But she kicked her booted feet as fast as she could—which admittedly likely wasn't all that fast—and clawed at the water.

There. Was she moving?

Below her, Elspeth fought, her hands grasping at Robena's wrist, and Robena had the thought the lassie was trying to get them *both* killed.

Well, forget that! One *of us is marrying Kester!*

Her.

'Twas going to be her.

When her free arm broke the surface of the loch, Robena was so surprised she almost stopped kicking. But then Elspeth jerked once more, and she remembered *she* was desperate for air as well, so she fought her way the last foot upward.

When her chin left the water, she sucked in a giant gulp of air and yanked as hard as she dared on Elspeth.

The lassie's head broke the surface of the water, but she didn't inhale. Frantic, Robena tried to force the girl higher, thinking that might help. It did nothing except shove *her* back under the water, and she came up spluttering, desperate, and confused as hell.

And then a strong pair of arms wrapped around her waist.

"I've got ye, lass," came Kester's smooth vow. "Ye're safe."

She *wanted* to turn in his arms and throw herself against him and sob helplessly in relief. But of course, she couldn't, because then stupid Elspeth really *would* drown.

"I've got the lassie," she gasped, trying to hold Elspeth upright. "She's no' breathing!"

"Grab her around the middle and squeeze," he commanded.

Since he was being obliging by holding her afloat, Robena did as he ordered.

At the same moment she wrapped her arms around the girl's chest, Kester hooked one arm under *her* arm and across *her* chest and began swimming. The jolting movement tightened her hold and—*St. Kelsi, thank ye!*—the girl jerked and began to retch.

As Kester pulled them both toward the place where the field sloped down to meet the loch, forming a little beach, Robena murmured soothingly to the girl. Elspeth coughed and spluttered, tears mixing with water from her adventure. Robena *wanted* to shake her and ask her how she could do something so stupid, but instead she promised over and over again that everything would be aright.

And it wasn't an empty vow. Everything *would* be aright. Kester had promised.

She felt the moment Kester's feet hit the bottom, because he was able to haul them mightily toward the shore. Robena heaved, and the lassie ended up on her hands and knees in the shallows, her gown and hair clinging pitifully to her.

St. Kelsi's eardrum, she's so young! What kind of Da uses a daughter that way?

But...her own father had decided all of his daughters would marry just to determine the next laird. Nay, their *wombs* would determine that.

Talk about stupid.

Kester's arm was around her waist, leading them both out of the shallows. "That was the *dumbest* thing I've ever seen!"

"I ken it!" She was breathing heavily but managed to pull

away from him and glare down at Elspeth. "I cannae believe ye'd do something that *stupid*."

"No' her," growled Kester. "*Ye*."

With a gasp, Robena whirled about, splashing water. Kester was standing with his fists on his hips, looking like some sort of avenging angel, with the water glistening across his wide chest and slicking back his hair.

Goodness, he was handsome, wasn't he? 'Twas hard to believe there was a lass out there who didn't want to marry him.

Focus. He just called ye stupid.

Oh, that's right. She sucked in another offended gasp and began to cough.

"Breathe, lass." He didn't sound amused.

"How— Ye think— Me? Ye think *I'm* stupid?"

There was genuine anger in his blue eyes. "I love ye, Robena!" he roared. "I love ye, and ye *deliberately* put yerself in danger!"

Her jaw dropped open. "Aye, of course I did!" She stomped toward him, one finger waving at his nose. "And I'll do it again!"

"If ye do it again, ye'll kill me!" He caught that finger, wrapping it in his large hand. "I *died*, watching ye jump off that cliff, ye mad woman!"

Since he hadn't lowered his voice, she didn't either, although she felt ridiculous standing there in the shallows in a soaking wet plaid, with a lassie retching behind her.

She shouted, "Let me make one thing perfectly clear, Kester MacBain! I will *always* jump off a cliff to save a child! And if ye think I'll be worried about *yer* feelings instead of the puir wee bairn when I do it, ye're mistaken!"

His frown had eased as she'd yelled at him, as had his shoulders. Now, he wasn't exactly smiling, but he wasn't frowning, either. With his hand still wrapped around her finger, he lifted it to his lips and brushed one kiss across her fingertip.

"Well then," he finally said, "I suppose I'll have to teach ye to swim, aye?"

"Aye!"

And then he was pulling and she was falling toward him, and their arms were around each other and the kiss was *desperate*, celebrating all they had and all they'd almost lost.

And it went on forever.

Or, at least until the Murrays skidded to a stop in the sand.

"*Elspeth!*" the old laird huffed, splashing out into the water to scoop up his daughter. "Elspeth, ye complete idiot, why would ye do something so dumb?"

Robena had pulled away enough to watch and opened her mouth to chastise Murray for such an insult...despite having thought the same thing moments ago.

But Laird Murray surprised her.

After bursting out with that harsh critique, he crushed wee Elspeth to his chest, raining kisses upon her crown, cradling her against him as if she were precious to him.

Obviously, she was.

For her part, the lassie was crying, her arms snaking around her father's neck, neither of them caring she was dripping all over his beard.

With haunted eyes, the laird looked over his daughter's head at Robena standing in Kester's arms. He was breathing heavily when he nodded to them.

"We have—have much to say to one another."

She felt Kester nod.

Murray nodded again, the movement jerky, as if he couldn't quite understand all that was happening. 'Twas as if the one thing he *could* be certain of was his hold on his daughter. He held the lassie as if he'd never let her go.

"Soon," he managed to say, half-turning away. "I must —Elspeth...."

"Aye, Murray," Kester said. "We'll meet ye at yer tent."

Another nod—more of a jerk of his chin—and Murray splashed toward his waiting men.

SHE FELT LIKE A DROWNED RAT.

A *happy* drowned rat.

Kester had saved her. He'd saved her, then he'd kissed her, and in between he'd roared out his love for her for everyone to hear.

Was it any wonder she was clinging to him as he led her through the encampment, one arm thrown around her shoulders?

"Everyone's staring at ye," he muttered darkly.

"Aye!" She beamed up at him. "I'm wearing a white shirt, Kester, and 'tis soaking wet."

He glanced down at her—or, more accurately, her tits— and with a muted growl, swept her off her feet and clasped her to his chest.

She giggled happily and pressed her cheek to his shoulder.

'Twas hard to follow his twisted stalk through the gathered clans, but he barely acknowledged the greetings and jests thrown his way. Before she knew it, he was releasing her, letting her slide down his body until she stood on her own feet, and she found they'd stopped before a small circle of even smaller tents.

Auld Gommy was crouched before a fire at the center. He slowly stood, his mouth agape as he took in her state.

Before he could comment on her half-nakedness, she planted her hands on her hips. "Auld Gommy MacBain! Have ye had *tents* in yer saddlebags all this time? And ye've made me sleep on the *ground?*"

Beneath his beard, his mouth was opening and closing.

Kester's hand closed around hers. "They thought ye a lad, remember."

"I'm no'." She smiled as she pointed one finger from her free hand at her tits.

Auld Gommy made a choking sound.

Kester growled again and tugged her toward one of the tents. "In here. Get changed. When we go see Murray and get this mess worked out, I'll no' have him—or anyone else—staring at what's mine."

'Twas rude. 'Twas demeaning. 'Twas definitely sexist—whatever that word meant.

So why did Robena's knees go all weak at the sound of his possessiveness?

She sent him a flirtatious smile as she ducked into the tent, hoping he'd be thinking of her stripping out of her wet clothing.

Unfortunately, that was much more difficult than expected, given the fact the tents really *were* miniscule. She could barely rest on her knees under the highest point, which meant she ended up getting changed while half-reclined.

This tent was definitely Kester's, and someone had placed her bags here as well. She ran her fingers lovingly over the strings of the lute before taking a deep breath and reaching for her yellow gown.

There was no use pretending any longer.

Everyone here knew wee Robbie Oliphant had tits, and she wouldn't be able to enter the Highland Piping Competition, which was due to start at sundown. So, she might as well embrace who she was.

The silk was difficult to pull on over her wet hair, but she managed. Of course, 'twas horribly wrinkled, but in the general scheme of things, she doubted anyone would be looking at her wrinkles.

She would stand proudly at Kester's side when he confronted the Murray, and she'd do it as herself.

And to hell with her reputation.

But before she clambered out of the tent, her hands dropped unbidden to the pipes. When her fingers closed around them, a jolt of energy passed through her.

This was who she was.

She was a lass, aye, but she was also a piper.

That sense of surety filled her, emboldened her. She took a deep breath and half-rolled, half-crawled out of Kester's tent. He was standing at the fire, his arms crossed and a heavy frown on his lips as he stared down at whatever Auld Gommy was cooking.

But when she emerged, his glance turned into a long, appreciative perusal, lingering on the pipes under her arm, and she knew she was making the right decision.

"Lass," he finally murmured in that tone which never failed to make her thighs clench, "ye look good enough to eat."

Since she could guess what he was referencing, Robena blushed. But she didn't look away; in fact, she smiled at him, hoping to tempt him into a kiss.

It worked.

He stalked closer, his hands settling on her hips before he tugged her closer, pulling her flush against him. He'd changed as well, into a dry plaid and shirt, although his hair looked as wild and curly as hers did.

"I'm proud to call ye mine, Robena Oliphant, nae matter what Murray or the King says. But I'll be even prouder that ye've decided to stand beside me as yer true self."

"Och, so ye dinnae want me to glue on another mustache?" she teased.

He responded by kissing her. 'Twas a deep, slow kiss,

exactly the kind she needed. It reminded her they were both still alive and had vowed to be together, somehow, someway.

When he finally pulled back, she was glad he had a hold on her hips, because she likely would've fallen flat on her face otherwise.

"There," he murmured, his gaze settling on her lips. "Now ye look as if ye *truly* belong to me. Let us go meet our future, eh?"

This walk through the encamped clans seemed to take much longer. Robena wasn't certain if 'twas because she knew what awaited them, or if Kester really was walking slower. It did seem as if he was constantly stopping to accept greetings this time, and each time he was shown respect and admiration from Highland lairds, her heart swelled a little.

By the time they made their way up the hill to the Murray camp, it seemed as if half the Highlands was trailing behind them, eager to see how this little drama would play out. Apparently, the story of Kester saving Laird Murray's daughter—after refusing to marry her—had swept through the Games.

Gossip was apparently far more interesting than the piping competitions, which were supposed to start at sundown, within the hour. She tucked her pipes under her arm, their familiar weight helping to ground her, remind her that everything would work out fine.

Hopefully.

Laird Murray wasn't waiting for them this time, but he emerged from the large tent before Kester had to call for him. He looked...smaller, somehow. Mayhap worry for his daughter had diminished him, and Robena found herself liking him all the more for that.

He nodded curtly, awkwardly, to Kester, before turning to Robena. He gave her a long stare, his gaze lingering on the hem of her gown and the pipes under her arm. Finally, Kester cleared his throat and the older man's head jerked, like a dog called to a whistle.

Mayhap Murray realized this because he scowled as he offered her a curt nod as well.

"This is Robena Oliphant," Kester announced, his fingers lacing through hers. No more, just her name. Mayhap he felt the gesture said enough.

When Murray's gaze dropped to their locked hands and he flushed again, Robena suspected it *had*.

That was the fortuitous moment for Lady Elspeth, she of the young and silly decisions, to step out of the tent. She wore a dry gown—blue this time—and was busy braiding her own hair. She marched up to her father and tilted her head back to glare up at him.

"Da, for the last time, I dinnae *want* to marry MacBain!"

Robena hid her smile, for the first time feeling sorry for Murray, who had to parent such a daughter.

Still, Murray growled, "Ye'll do what I say!"

St. Kelsi help us, we're back to this?

Elspeth stomped her foot as she finished off the braid. "I willnae marry MacBain!"

Robena spoke up. "Ye cannae marry MacBain."

As the girl turned, a thankful smile on her face, her father frowned. "She cannae?"

"She cannae," agreed Kester, obviously hiding his amusement.

Robena shrugged and held up their joined hands. "Sorry, Lady Elspeth. Ye cannae marry Kester MacBain, because *I'm* marrying him."

Kester nodded and hauled her closer. "She is. She's verra determined."

A smile bloomed across Elspeth's face as Laird Murray shook his head. "Ye...ye're marrying my enemy? But ye saved my daughter, Robena."

"*Lady* Robena," Kester corrected smugly. "One of the Oliphant's daughters. Soon to be Lady MacBain, nae matter what ye have to say about it."

Murray ignored him and lowered his hand to his daughter's shoulder. Stiffly, he bowed to Robena. "Milady, we—myself, my daughter, my clan—are in yer debt. Thanks to yer brave actions, my Elspeth lives."

And her eyes widened in horror as she realized what he was saying.

She didn't want him beholden to *her*. Quickly, she whirled and shoved her pipes toward Pudge, who took them without hesitation. Then she took a deep breath and raised her free finger. She made her tone harsh when she pinned Murray with a glare.

"'Twas phenomenally stupid of Elspeth to go over the side of that cliff. However, 'twas even stupider for *me* to go after her." As the older man blinked at her, she shook her head. "I cannae swim. I grabbed her, aye, but if Kester hadn't come for both of us, we'd both be drowned."

She turned her attention to Kester, only to find him smiling down at her. Still speaking to Murray, she softened her tone a bit. "Ye owe Laird MacBain yer thanks, no' me."

Kester's grin turned soft and he raised their joined hands to his lips, pressing a kiss across the back of her knuckles. Slowly, he released her hand, only to snake his arm around her shoulders and pull her against him. She thought—*hoped?*—he might drop a kiss to her lips, but instead, he turned them both to Murray.

Expectantly.

The older laird was frowning as he switched his gaze back and forth between the pair of them, and Robena found herself holding her breath...*praying* he'd make no more fuss. *Praying* he saw what he owed Kester.

'Twas Elspeth who saved the day.

The lassie slipped her small hand in one of her father's. She smiled sweetly—St. Kelsi help them, she was used to getting her way, wasn't she?—and bobbed a brief curtsey. "Thank ye, Laird MacBain, for saving my life."

Of course, she completely ignored Robena, the one whom she'd kicked and punched during the life-saving process...but since Robena wanted the attention on Kester, she thought she could manage to forgive the lass.

Her father heaved a great sigh and rolled his eyes, possibly at his own stubbornness.

"Ye're right." He switched his glare to Kester. "My daughter's right." He offered his hand, and, to his credit, only looked half-reluctant. "I—my clan—owe ye our thanks, MacBain."

Kester stepped away from her to accept the offered hand, clasping forearms with the man who'd been his enemy for so long. The two men wore equally stoic expressions. Robena knew Kester's hid uncertainty—not daring to hope Murray was being serious. Did the other man, as well?

Wee Elspeth spoke up again. "I'm *no'* marrying him, Da."

As Kester stepped back and took Robena's hand once more, Murray shook his head. "Ye cannae, lassie." He winked at Robena. "One of yer saviors will be marrying the man." He took a deep breath, then nodded once more to Kester. "As far as I'm concerned, MacBain, we're nae longer enemies. And if it'll get ye to quit bedeviling me, I'll grant ye Kester's Meadow. As a wedding gift."

'Twas possible he said more after that, but Robena didn't hear it, because Kester let out a mighty whoop. Before she could blink, he'd grabbed her around the waist and was spinning her in a circle, and the thunderous cheers of the gathered crowd nearly deafened her.

And she was smiling so wide tears came to her eyes.

Or mayhap they were tears of joy.

All she knew was he was beaming up at her, as if he'd just been handed everything he'd ever wanted.

Mayhap he had.

For certes, 'twas exactly the way she felt, as well.

In the distance, a piper began a cheerful tune.

Kester dropped a quick kiss to her lips, over and done far too quickly to celebrate the joy pounding through her veins. But his grin was full of promise, and she knew she had tonight —and all the nights of their lives—to look forward to more kisses.

"Well, soon-to-be-wife? Shall I escort ye to the piping competition? Show them what a lass can do?"

Grinning, she slipped her arm through his and took the pipes Pudge offered her. She lifted her chin. "I think that sounds like a fine idea, my love."

CHAPTER 11

"Are ye disappointed?" Pudge asked, wearing his usual scowl.

Kester, who stood beside the priest with his arms crossed in front of his chest, raised a brow at his friend. "'Tis a fine day in the Highlands, the MacBains will have Kester's Meadow returned to them, and I'm about to marry the woman I love. Why would I be disappointed?"

One of Pudge's shoulders jerked, a subtle shrug. "She didnae win."

Ah.

Grinning—there wasn't anything which could stop him from grinning today—Kester swept his gaze around the representatives of the various clans who were attending his wedding.

Last night, the piping competition had lasted until the embers burned low, then had erupted again this morning. At first, the stodgy traditionalists had been reluctant to allow Robena to compete, but 'twas Murray who'd surprised them.

The grumpy old laird had stomped into the center of the piping circle and declared, "Then dinnae let her compete, but let her *play.* I think she's proven she can do aught a lad can do, eh?"

Since the story of her daring—and stupid—attempt to rescue wee Elspeth Murray had already swept through the gathered clans, there were few who could object.

And so, Robena, despite her exhaustion, despite her near drowning, had played.

And Kester's grin grew even wider, remembering.

She'd held his gaze as she'd piped, and her song had been one of celebration, one of joy. The notes tripped fast and fun from her fingers, each chasing the next in a sound of pure delight.

The Sutherland piper had countered with a dirge, and the MacLeod with a march, and she'd answered them all with the same aching, mournful tune she'd played for the MacBain men days ago.

Kester wasn't the only one wiping at his eyes when she finished.

By this morning, when everyone gathered again on the main field, only a few pipers were left. The others had removed themselves from the competition one by one as they realized they weren't as talented. Eventually, only Robena and the Mackenzie piper—a grizzled old grandda of a man with a beard as long as Auld Gommy's—remained.

And when the final note was played, the Mackenzie piper offered her his hand, clasping it as if they were equals.

"Laird?" Pudge prompted.

Remembering the question, Kester shrugged. "Did she no' win?"

"'Tis being said the Mackenzie won the competition."

"Mayhap, but he—and every other man here—saw and heard her skill, and kens she's their equal. That was what she wanted." 'Twas what he'd wanted too.

Pudge hummed, half-thoughtful, half-surprised. "True. So ye're saying the actual title doesnae matter?"

"No' to her. No' to me. And no' to all the pipers who heard and acknowledged her."

His friend grunted. "Ye ken, ye're smarter than ye look, Laird."

The insult surprised a laugh out of Kester, and as he watched, Pudge's lips reluctantly curled upward.

In the distance, a single, clear pipe note began. As the attention of the gathered men swung toward the hill, more notes—more pipers—joined in.

And Kester didn't think his smile could grow, but he was wrong.

Heralded by their music, the best pipers of the Highlands began to march in step down the rise where the Murrays had camped. And in the middle of their honor guard marched a phalanx of MacBains: Mook in the front, Weesil in the back, and Auld Gommy and Giric flanking.

And in the middle…

In the middle of his men and the Highlands' best pipers, marched Lady Robena Oliphant.

Kester was already moving, striding toward the newcomers. But before he reached them, the pipers split and spread out, moving to stand around the inside of the circle the gathered clan representatives had formed.

And as the MacBains came to a stop, a small figure in a blue dress ran up.

'Twas Elspeth Murray, and she held an armful of wildflowers.

Kester watched Robena's smile grow as she pulled the lassie into a hug, then chuckled when the girl scolded her for crushing the flowers. Robena took the bouquet in one arm, and Elspeth's hand in her other, and the pair of beauties turned to face Kester and the men.

His heart swelled with pride as her chin lifted and she marched toward him, proving to everyone watching how happy she was to become his wife.

He met her at the edge of the circle and leaned in close enough so the nearest men—they were wearing Sutherland plaid, but he didn't recognize them—couldn't hear.

"Are ye certain, Robena?" he murmured.

She seemed surprised. "About marrying ye?"

"About marrying me without yer father's permission. About marrying me *today, here,* instead of waiting to get back to MacBain Castle."

Her smile softened, and she pushed herself up on her toes to brush a kiss across his cheek.

"Of course, I'm certain, my love. Da approved of ye as a match for me; 'twas just Murray we needed to convince."

"And the King." He shrugged ruefully.

"Laird Murray says—"

Wee Elspeth interrupted. "My da has already drafted a letter to the King, explaining we're now allies with the MacBains, and as such, *I* get to choose my *own* husband, instead of being handed over like a sack of peas in exchange for some stupid meadow."

Robena's expression went curiously blank as she inclined her head regally. "Aye, as it should be."

"So." The girl hefted a big sigh and tossed her hair. "Ye two can marry with Da's blessing. And the King's, too. Da is *verra* good friends with him, ye ken."

Kester's brow rose. "I ken," he managed blandly.

When Robena's attention turned back to him, she was smiling again, but teasingly. "So ye see, Laird MacBain, I've nae objection to marrying ye *here* and *now*. My father approves of the match and we've two dozen Highland chieftains standing as witnesses." Her wink was exaggerated. "The only concern is that if ye're unlucky to sire a son on me immediately, ye might end up as laird of the Oliphants as well."

His heart began to pound faster at the thought of Robena's belly swelling with their child. "I think—I think 'tis a risk I dinnae mind so much."

He offered her his arm, and as she slid her hand through it, he heard Giric mutter, "Nay, *sex*, ye big oaf. They're speaking of *sex*."

"Aaaah," Mook rumbled. "'Tis my favorite part!"

Robena began to chuckle, and Kester followed. Laughing, he gently tugged her across the circle, toward the waiting men.

Here and now.

And forever.

ROBENA HADN'T STOPPED SMILING all evening. As the sounds of the wedding celebration faded behind them and they headed into the woods, she tucked herself up against Kester's side, twining both sets of fingers through one of his.

He carried a torch in his other hand but turned to send her a worried glance. "Ye must be exhausted, lass. We'll give ye a few days to rest afore we—"

"Kester MacBain," she interrupted, knowing good and well what he was hinting at. "I am fine. I am *more* than fine. If ye think ye can use that wee bit of excitement yesterday to get out of yer husbandly duties tonight…"

Apparently, her threatening tone wasn't all that threatening. With a chuckle, he stepped into the little clearing and tossed the torch toward a fire ring someone had set up. The kindling flared to life, revealing a small tent, just as he pulled her into his arms.

He rested his chin on her head, his arms around her waist. *"Husbandly duties*, eh?"

Just having him this close was intoxicating. He'd bathed sometime today—not just the impromptu dip in the loch he'd taken yesterday, but an actual bath, complete with soap and a shave and whatever other manly things men did in the bath.

He smelled delightful.

"I love ye," she whispered against his neck, her lips skimming his skin. "And I dinnae want to sleep yet. I want ye inside of me, husband."

Perhaps he wasn't as unaffected as he was trying to be, because his hips gave a sort of involuntary jerk at her words— or mayhap the touch of her lips—and his hardness pressed against her belly.

"Robena," he groaned, "ye ought to have a fine bed for yer wedding night. No' a simple tent and a few blankets."

"Nonsense." She kissed his collarbone, then lower. "I will have ye to keep me warm. And I plan on sleeping atop ye tonight, husband, and that cannae be any softer than the ground."

In case he misunderstood her meaning, she reached between them and cupped his hardness. The noise he made was a sort of strangled, hopeless laugh.

"I'm beginning to suspect ye just like calling me *husband*, lass."

"Och, well, husband, I've waited long enough, have I no'? I'm entitled to it, husband. For certes, husband, the novelty of 'twill wear off, husband, in a year or two. Husband."

Chuckling now, he captured her lips in his.

Likely, just to shut her up.

With a moan of her own, she wrapped her arm around his neck and held on, while her other hand caressed him through the MacBain kilt.

"Do ye ken how much I love this gown?" he murmured, while his lips trailed hot kisses along her jaw and down her throat. "This yellow silk? It makes ye look… God's Wounds, Robena!"

Since she'd squeezed him involuntarily in response to the way he'd cupped her breast through the fabric, she thought she could be forgiven.

"How?" she gasped. "How does it make me look?"

"Like a *lady*," he admitted with a chuckle. "Like a gift. Like a fine piece of pottery. God Almighty, I want to unwrap ye with my teeth."

His metaphors needed a little help, but since he was currently attempting to unlace her gown while his lips were still on her, she decided *he* could be forgiven as well.

So, all she said was, "Let me help." This was, after all, the only gown she'd packed.

'Twas a slow process, one frequently interrupted by kisses and touches and a growing desperation.

But soon enough, she was naked, spread out atop the blankets stacked in the tent, and he was crawling in as well. Mayhap 'twas the position she was lying in—leaning back, supported by her elbows, her heels on the ground and her knees spread—which gave him the idea, but a speculative look came to his eyes.

"Kest—?" was all she managed before, with no warning, he lowered his mouth to the junction of her thighs.

Oh.

This was…

This was…

Well, Robena's mind was curiously, deliciously blank, so if asked, she'd have to say *This was bleeeeerrrrgggghahblaff.* That was more or less how she felt.

With a sigh, she allowed her legs to fall open as Kester's tongue swept along her core.

St. Kelsi protect her, but the man was *amazing*!

She'd spent her life learning the art of music; she knew a person's tongue could be capable of trilling, of whistling, of forming high and low notes, of controlling the melody played on a flute or pipe.

But she'd never realized a tongue could do *this.*

Unbidden, her hands fell to his head, her fingers curling through his locks, holding him in place. He hummed against her, a little laugh which she felt throughout her entire body. Her hips bucked in response, which caused him to chuckle again, and then his finger slid into her.

"That's it, lass," he murmured against her slickness. "That's a good girl. Ye like that?"

Oh, St. Kelsi's eardrums, did she *ever*! With a needy sort of mewling sound—which might've been embarrassing to admit under any other circumstances—Robena planted her weight on her heels and pressed her arse off the blankets, trying to get closer to the object of such pleasure.

Mayhap, if her body hadn't already been so desperate for him, this would've taken longer. But as 'twas, she felt her orgasm building behind her core, each gentle ministration of his tongue—his teeth! His lips!—sending her ever closer.

"So soft," he murmured. "So wet. So wet for me."

"Aye!" she gasped, squeezing her eyes shut. "Kester, *aye.*"

He was being so gentle, as if knowing her nerve-endings were raw with need. 'Twas that consideration, more than anything else, which sent her over the edge.

Well, *that,* and the fact he happened to close his lips around her clitoris at that exact moment.

So really, it was *that.* And the fact he slid an extra finger into her. *And* the consideration.

And really, all of that together? She was powerless to resist.

With a gasp, she arched against his mouth as her pleasure burst over her, bright colors swirling behind her eyes. She bucked, but he continued his torture, and then he hummed.

And really, how was a woman supposed to handle a man as desirable as Kester *humming*?

She screamed his name.

The colors continued, but she remembered to breathe, and after a thousand pounding heartbeats, she felt herself beginning to come back down to earth.

That was when Kester pulled his fingers from inside her, lifted his head, and crawled up her body.

Really, there wasn't any other way to describe it; one moment, he was lying between her thighs, supping at her, and the next, he was looming over her, his weight braced on one hand as the other stroked his cock.

"I cannae hold back, Robena," he gasped.

She wrapped her arms around his neck and pulled him closer. "I dinnae want ye to."

When he plunged into her wet opening, they both sucked in a joyful gasp.

"Hold onto me, lass," he commanded, and *of course* she was going to obey.

His motions were no longer gentle, and that was perfectly fine with her. His frantic need had re-kindled her own. Or mayhap her pleasure had never ceased.

The throbbing in her core grew once more, with each shuddering thrust, and she flattened her palms against his wide shoulders, urging him on.

Her pleasure was building, building, building….

And then he stiffened and groaned. She pulled him down, her lips seeking his. As he claimed her with a kiss, she felt a warm flood against her womb. Almost unconsciously, her feet wrapped around his calves, and she *squeezed*.

All it took was one more thrust from him—his way made slick by his tongue, her desire, and his seed—before she was soaring over the edge once more.

"Kester!" she gasped against his mouth, and he hummed in response.

Robena's pleasure pulsed in ever-decreasing beats, each one softer and longer than the last, until she could suck in a breath without the worry of swallowing her tongue.

Finally, she collapsed back onto the blankets, taking him with her. His head pillowed between her breasts, she listened to the sounds of his breathing and smiled into the darkness.

After a long while, Kester stirred. "I suppose a tent isnae the worst place to spend a wedding night."

"Aye," she teased, her fingers stroking his hair. "Although I confess I'm looking forward to a fine bed in MacBain Castle."

He lifted his head. "So nae more bathing in lochs together?"

"Och, husband!" she smacked him playfully. "I was going to suggest we do that this verra night."

"Ye'd be too cold."

"Ye'd keep me warm," she countered.

Kester rose on his elbows. "Ye cannae swim."

"Ye will keep me safe."

She could hear his smile when he drawled, "Aye, that is true enough."

Robena wrapped her arms around his waist as he moved over her. "And when we bathe, ye can make certain to get my tits *really* clean."

He burst into laughter.

Feeling mischievous, and already hoping for a repeat of the pleasure she'd just received, she wriggled her hips under his. "I'll likely have to hold tightly onto ye. Mayhap wrap my legs around ye." She shifted under him. "Ye ken, in order to protect me from drowning."

"Really, lass?" Still chuckling, he rolled to one side, then propped his head up on his hand. "I'm thinking all this talk of bathing might just be an excuse to get me naked and in yer arms again."

Robena gasped theatrically. "Ye think I would do such a thing?"

"For more pleasure?"

Remembering the way the MacBain warriors had spoken of sex, when they thought her a lad, she kept her tone solemn when she nodded. "The *aaahhhh* is my favorite part."

"Saints protect us," he groaned, dropping his head down with a dull *thunk*. "My men have corrupted ye."

"Thoroughly," she agreed with a giggle, rolling over atop him. "I learned so much from them, and I think ye can teach me even more."

In the dim light, she saw him peek out from under his forearm. "Like what?" he asked suspiciously.

She could feel his half-erect member, sticky with his seed. Mischievously, she closed her hand around it. "Have ye ever heard of *The Supplicant Swan*, husband?"

Her only response was a strained sort of grunt, and she smiled.

"It involves a man in this position, and a woman bending over him, her head and neck bobbing as she takes his cock into her mouth—"

He sat up. "How do ye ken such a thing?"

"I spent a lot of time as a lad, remember?" She teased. "I was thinking I'd like to try *The Supplicant Swan*, but after we've bathed."

He was moving before she'd finished her sentence, pulling her out of the tent. Laughing, she called, "Where are we going, husband?"

"To bathe!"

As they rose to their feet, she teased, "And after, I could reaffix my mustache while we practiced—"

Her mock threat was cut short by her squeal when he—as naked as she—hoisted her over his shoulder.

"What are ye doing?" she half-squeaked, half-laughed.

He lightly smacked her arse-cheek, which caused her laugh to turn a little breathless, especially when he turned the touch into a caress.

"Kester?" she breathed.

He was already crashing through the woods and she admired his sense of surety. Especially without boots.

"I'm taking ye to bathe, wife. I figured this was the easiest way to get to the *aaahhh*, without a mustache."

She propped her elbows up on his back, planted her chin in her hands, and decided to enjoy the ride. From this angle, she could see his arse-dimples in the moonlight.

"Well, love, far be it for me to object to yer plan."

"I love ye, Robbie."

And she began to laugh.

Really, what more could a lass ask for?

EPILOGUE

"Oh, this is terrible. Just terrible."

Since Mother's refrain hadn't changed much in the hour since she'd come into the solar to "help," Nicola felt justified in ignoring her. Instead, she tried to block out the older woman's mumbles and pacing and hand-wringing and concentrate on her measurements.

Should she bring a full measure of wormwood, or would a half-measure do?

The nunnery would likely have it in their herb garden, but could she trust them to have dried it properly for use?

Oh, St. Crystal's retina, 'tis no' as if ye dinnae have room in yer bags for an extra handful.

Mind made up, Nicola carefully poured more of the herb into the pouch, then hefted it. Aye, 'twould do. Besides, how much trouble could a cohort of nuns get into, really? 'Twas unlikely she'd have to deal with stab wounds and whatnot.

On the other hand, Coira *was* escorting her….

Lips curling wryly, Nicola slid the pouch of wormwood into the pile of supplies to secure to her saddle.

"Just terrible. *Terrible.* How could ye do this to me? Yer own mother? I birthed ye, I raised ye, I cared for ye…."

Nicola managed to refrain from snorting as she turned back to hear weights and measures on her worktable.

More like I cared for ye.

"And now my darling daughter is preparing to *abandon* me most cruelly, just when I need her most!"

With a sigh, Nicola rounded on her mother, her hands on her hips. "And *why* do ye need me? In particular, right now? What is wrong this time?"

Mother was wringing her hands in front of her. With a completely serious expression, she announced, "My collapsing malaria is acting up again."

Collapsing malaria?

Collapsing malaria?

Only years of experience treating Mother's ridiculous ailments kept Nicola from reacting. She might've *wanted* to sigh meaningfully, pinch the bridge of her nose, and shake her head. She *could've* thrown up her hands and shouted, "Ye complete imbecile, ye cannae just slap two words together and claim ye suffer from it! No' when *I'm* busy suffering from *ye!*"

But she didn't, because she'd learned Mother's tears were worse than her collapsing malaria. Or screaming lupus. Or, that one time, cow herpes.

So instead, Nicola managed to keep wearing her "healer face," as Coira called it; the calm and empathetic expression she'd perfected for when it came time to meet a new patient.

Or an old one.

"Aright, Mother. I'll make certain to leave plenty of rosemary." She'd convinced Mother years ago that rosemary could cure most ailments. "All ye need to do is mix it with some honey water and whisky whenever ye feel a bout of—of collapsing malaria coming on." St. Crystal protect her, 'twas difficult to keep a straight face. "As always, it'll protect ye."

"Will that be enough?" Still, with the handwringing.

Nicola stifled her sigh and shook her head as she turned back to her herbs. "I promise."

Mother wailed, "How could ye do this to me?"

"Me?" Giving up on *calm and empathetic*, Nicola whirled to pierce her mother with a glare. "How could *I* do this to ye?

The older woman was still pacing, the skirt of her blue gown swishing around her. For the first time, Nicola noticed her mother *was* looking frailer, her shoulders and her hands thinner and more delicate than they used to be.

"How could ye go off and leave me, Nicola?" Mother sniffed. "How could ye even *consider* it?"

Nicola reached for her mother, pulling her into her arms on her next pass. When had she grown taller than the woman who'd birthed her? Mayhap 'twas just that Mother *seemed* smaller these days. She tucked the older woman against her shoulder.

"Ye kenned this day was coming, Mother," she said gently. "Da declared we must all be married, after all."

"Married is different from taking holy vows!" the older woman wailed, her voice devolving into sniffles.

"Is it?" Nicola murmured, running a soothing hand up and down her mother's back. "Either would mean no' being here at Oliphant Castle." *At yer beck and call.* She loved her mother, she truly did...but she had a life of her own she wanted to lead. "And if I took vows, I wouldnae be tied to one—man."

She almost said *person*, thinking of how much her mother had relied on her over the years, and how exhausting that had become. Marriage would be equally exhausting, Nicola was certain; having to devote one's life to one's husband, and just hope they were worth it.

Nay, her plan was better.

"Marriage to Christ isnae the better choice, daughter."

Nicola managed to shrug, despite her mother hanging on her. "'Twill be easier to marry a man long dead—"

"He is Risen!"

"Och, aye, 'tis what I meant." Nicola awkwardly patted her mother's back. "But He isnae *here*, which makes Him a lot easier to marry. Serve. Whatever." If she took vows, she'd be able to help a whole host of people with her healing skills, not just her mother and the occasional sick Oliphant. "Besides, I'm no' *definitely* taking vows, Mother. I just said I'm planning on discussing it with the Mother Superior when I'm at the nunnery."

"But ye're *definitely* leaving me," the older woman wailed.

Nicola felt safe rolling her eyes. "Well, *Christ*."

"Exactly!"

That was the moment Coira chose to come stamping into the solar, thank St. Crystal. She wore braies and a man's tunic, and a pair of saddlebags were thrown over her shoulder.

"What the hell's taking so—*oh*."

Her gaze landed on Mother, still sniffling against Nicola's shoulder. The sisters exchanged a look only years of commiserating could achieve.

It plainly said, *Can ye believe this shite?*

Nicola cleared her throat. "Mother is concerned about me leaving."

"'Tis no' forever."

"If she takes vows, *'twill* be!" their mother wailed.

With a shake of her head, Coira began to gather up the herb packages Nicola had prepared, stuffing them into the bags she carried. "She's no' taking vows, Mother. She just needs to get away from here and from Da's stupid ultimatum."

Ridiculously hopeful, Mother straightened fast enough to pop her spine, and Nicola winced, knowing she'd complain about that, too.

"Ye mean it, Coira? Ye'll bring her back?"

Coira, as the eldest, had the strength and discipline both their parents lacked. She turned and held Mother's pleading look. "Nay, I'll no'. If Nik wants to stay with the nuns at St. Dorcas the Ever Petulant for a while and tend to the ill there, I'll no' stop her; but I'll be returning home." She turned back to her work and finished in a mutter, "I cannae trust Doughall to handle the clan's business properly while I'm away."

No one who knew the Oliphants would be surprised Coira had entrusted the Commander with her usual duties, rather than turning them back over to their father, bless him.

Nicola gently set her mother away from her. "Thank ye for caring for me, but ye dinnae need to fret. I swear I'll no' abandon ye, Mother. If I *do* decide to take vows, I'll arrange to send medicines and herbs to ye fortnightly."

"Ye swear?"

And no one who knew the Oliphants would be surprised by the fact Mother didn't protest she'd miss Nicola for *herself*... Nay, they'd all know Lady Oliphant's litany of ailments—mostly imaginary—were the focus of her life.

"I swear, Mother," Nicola sighed.

The older woman sniffled into her handkerchief. "First Robena runs off, now ye. Wynda and Fen at least married and stayed here on Oliphant land."

'Twas Coira who interrupted, dismissive of what she considered nonsense. "Robena is chasing down her laird, and when she catches up with him, she'll work out that shite about MacBain being betrothed to another woman, and she'll marry him. Dinnae fash, Mother—she's fine." Coira shrugged as she tied the bags closed. "I mean, she'll be on MacBain land once she becomes his wife, but she'll be safe."

"And Leanna—" Mother began.

"Is on McClure land," Coira finished. "Happily married, and likely making Da a grandson." Only her sisters—Nicola being the only one in the room—could hear the bitterness in her voice. "So, Nicola leaving for the nunnery for a bit isnae any different than Leanna and Robbie leaving ye."

Before their mother could respond, Coira swung the full saddlebags up onto her shoulder once more. Her smile was mocking and her tone vicious when she announced, "But dinnae fash, ye'll always have *me*."

Mother heard it this time and likely knew why her eldest objected to their father's scheme. So, she sighed and shook her head, before reaching for Nicola once more.

This time her hug was quick and perfunctory. Then she straightened. "Ye'll write to me? Tell me how ye fare and what yer decision is?"

There was a lump in Nicola's throat, but she managed to nod jerkily.

Mother waved the kerchief and turned away, already sniffling again. "Then go. Godspeed. Hurry back."

Nicola's arms ached to reach across the space, to pull her mother into another hug. How much of that urge, however, was part of her drive to comfort those around her?

And how much was it the need of a lass who just wanted to be loved for herself, rather than what she could do?

So, she exchanged glances with her sister and pretended not to see the pity in Coira's eyes. With a sigh, Nicola looked around the women's solar, which had been part of her domain for so long.

Then she turned and followed her sister out for what might be the last time.

Mother didn't call out, and Nicola told herself it didn't matter.

At the Abbey of St. Dorcas the Ever Petulant, she could do more good for more people, and that was what was important.

AUTHOR'S NOTE

AUTHOR'S NOTE
On Historical Accuracy

Okay, we're four books into the *Bad in Plaid* series, after eight books of *Hots for Scots*. Point is: you shouldn't be surprised by my particular brand of…how shall we say it? *Je ne sais quoi?*

Nah, I can *sais quoi*. It's "playing fast and loose with historical facts" that's what *sais quoi*.

(Also, apparently, playing fast and loose with French translations….)

What I'm saying is, I like messing around with the "facts" and the tropes we've come to expect from medieval Scottish romances. But there *are* places (believe it or not), where I *do* make shite up.

I know, I know, it's hard to believe. I'll wait while you get your smelling salts.

<whistles nonchalantly>

Okay, you're back? Then let's get started.

The trope of the King ordering two warring clans to unite through marriage is as old as Scottish romance and doesn't really need investigating here. It's often a great basis for an enemies-to-lovers plot, and I hope you laughed a bit at how I turned it on its head. (Although let's be clear: plenty of girls were married at age seven in the medieval period to cement alliances. We're modern ladies, though, and can laugh at that ridiculousness.)

So, in terms of what we actually need to discuss in this book....

First, and most importantly, is the whole female-piper-at-the-Highland-Games-thing.

But in order for me to explain why the premise (only men being allowed to compete) is bullshite, I have to back up a bit and talk about the Highland Games themselves, and how my interpretation of them is also, well, bullshite.

So, we've all read books which feature the Highland Games, and yes, they're a popular trope. In medieval romance, the Games are the times that warring clans put aside their differences and come together in good-natured competition, such as hurling logs at one another and dancing around swords.

But...the Highland Games we're thinking of are almost certainly a modern invention. See, after Bonnie Prince Charlie's failed uprising of 1745, the British Parliament enacted the Act of Proscription. This Act was aimed at breaking the power of the Highland clans and forcing the Scots—in particular, the Highlanders—to assimilate.

It sorta worked.

The most famous remnant of this Act, at least in terms of Scottish romance, was the outlawing of the clan tartan. (As I've said in other Author's Notes on historical accuracy: I completely ignore this. Yes, everyone knows medieval Scots didn't wear kilts. Do I care? No. It's a trope now and I'm rolling with it, because dudes in kilts with swords are *hot*.)

Okay, so, after the Act of Proscription was repealed in

1782, there was a slow resurgence of interest in Scottish history. During the forty years the Act was in place, gatherings and customs were forbidden, and so many of the old ways had been forgotten (which was, let's be honest, the whole damn point of the Act).

But the Highland Games became a *thing*.

By the early nineteenth century, it was common for each town/city to have their own version of the Games, and there were several national versions. The most famous gathering is in Braemar in September of each year, but the tradition of the annual games has spread throughout the world.

So, wait, Caroline...The Highland Games are a modern invention? Well...yes and no.

Way to hedge yer bets there, lass.

The annual competition and gathering we think of is more modern than not, but it has its basis in history. The earliest games are thought to have originated some four thousand years ago in Ireland, but for our purpose, I'll focus on Scotland. And, well...the Highlands.

There *is* evidence for competitive gatherings. One famous one occurred in the 1000s, when King Malcolm III hosted footraces (up a mountain near Braemar, because, of course) to determine who the fastest warrior was and thus who would become his royal messenger. Similar competitions occurred when a king or chieftain needed to choose personal guards, couriers, or warriors.

After all, what better way to choose the best and strongest dude than to gather all the dudes together and let them whale on each other until there's only one left standing?

#SimplifiedHistory

Okay, so there *were* competitive gatherings, which we might as well call "Highland Games", but they didn't occur with any sort of regularity. They did, however, almost certainly include piping, drumming, fiddling, and harping (where "harping" in that context means "to play a harp." I dunno if it's a real word; I made it up), as they do today.

Which finally—*finally*—brings us to our original point: There's no evidence that women weren't allowed to compete in medieval games. Why? Well, mainly because there's no such thing as a standardized "medieval Highland Games", much less a list of rules about them.

But I think it should be pretty obvious why I established that women were forbidden from participating in this time-line: how *else* was I going to have a cross-dressing trope in this book? I needed an excuse!

(Note: this trope is one of my all-time-favorites. If a book includes a heroine having to dress as a boy, I will immediately pick it up. I recently heard this trope called "chicks in pants" and I like that description a lot more than "cross-dressing"... the only problem, of course, is that Robena *isn't* wearing pants. I had a lot of fun with that; the idea that as a lad, she was wearing what was basically a more revealing skirt. Her *knees* were showing. *Gasp.*)

Moving on.…

Remember way back in chapter two, when Nicola teases Robena about drawing hearts all around the name "Lady Robena MacBain"? This was, of course, supposed to mock our experiences with Trapper Keepers and glitter pens in middle school when we fell in love for the first time. But one of my readers asked about the heart symbol, so I get to put on a history hat and explain.

Ahem.

The heart symbol has been around since antiquity, but historians and archaeologists agree that for centuries it just represented certain leaves. Think about it; there are leaves all over the world which are vaguely heart-shaped, and some of those plants are considered aphrodisiacs or associated with sex. So, it's possible that although this shape represented a plant, it *also* represented some aspect of love.

Meanwhile, in the western world, the heart—the organ in the middle of your chest—was coming to be associated with emotions like love. But it wasn't until the thirteenth century that we see evidence linking all three of these things—the organ, the symbol, the emotion—together. Even then, the depictions are ambiguous and up for interpretation. It wasn't until the late Middle Ages that we can say the heart symbol became unquestioningly linked with *love*.

I've been purposefully vague about the time period of the *Bad in Plaid* books, but we can guess they're somewhere in between the first evidence that maybe hearts are being linked to love and the point at which they definitely are. Hence Nicola's teasing.

Finally, I wanted to give a quick shout-out to medieval bathing, if only because of that really hot first scene between Kester and Robena in the loch. Now, loch-bathing is a fabulous trope in medieval Scottish romance, and I'm definitely not poo-pooing it. Sexy times are fun times! But how are these people actually bathing?

Well, the easiest (and most natural) way to bathe is one we actually saw in that scene: grab some sand and rub it all over. The scouring process will remove dirt and sweat...and also, bonus, the top layer of skin, any stains, and possibly even tattoos if you rub hard enough, *ha*!

But it's not like our characters didn't have and use soap. If you follow me on social media, you might know that I'm an amateur soap-maker (amateur in that I love doing it, but don't sell it), so this is a topic I know and love!

Soap-making is basically the process (called saponification) of bonding oils and alkalis together, which results in a solid chunk of soap. This soap has two main elements: it bonds to grease, and it dissolves in water (both necessary when it comes to, you know, actually removing grease from skin).

In modern soap-making, I would start with lye, mix it with water (my lye-water solution is very caustic and can be dangerous), then mix it with a certain amount and percentage of various oils (olive, grapeseed, castor, coconut, sustainably sourced palm, etc.).

Medieval soap-making had the same basic elements: an oil and an alkali. But they were made differently. First of all, the oils used weren't the posh ones I mentioned above. They would've almost certainly used the leftover animal fat that couldn't go into food-processing. Of course, fancy households used fancier imported oils and scented the soaps with various natural elements.

In order to make the lye water solution, they couldn't just order their lye from Amazon, as I do. They had to sift and clean wood ash, then pour boiling hot water on top of them and let them sit for a day. Then lime and more boiling water would be poured into that solution. After another day, they'd have what was essentially their lye water solution.

I love this bit of history, because it's so *scientific*! Like, can you imagine the earliest humans to work out how to create soap? The wrong wood ash, the wrong amount of water, the wrong order...and you wouldn't have a solution that was alkali enough to react with the oils. And then the combination of how much of the lye water to add to the oils...it would've involved years of guesswork and trial and error, and it's one aspect of social history which just fascinates me!

Our ancestors were pretty neat, ya know?

So, anyhow, that's medieval soap-making. Join me next time when I climb up on my soap box (Heh. See what I did there?) where I get passionate about some other miniscule thing no one else cares about!

Now that we've covered everything you need to know

about Robena and Kester, what's going on with Nicola? Is she *really* going to become a nun? What's she going to do at the Abbey of St. Dorcas the Ever Petulant?

And who, do you suppose, is she going to run into there?

Keep reading for a sneak peek of *A Plaid Case of Loving Ye*!

But first, I want to offer you a personal invitation to my reader group. If you're on Facebook, I hope you'll consider joining. It's where I post all the best book news first, and you'll be able to get to know me personally. My Cohort is also instrumental in helping me name characters and choose covers (they even suggested titles for this series)! So stop on by!

And now for Nicola and her mystery man…

SNEAK PEEK

From *A Plaid Case of Loving Ye*

The convent of St. Dorcas the Ever Petulant sat on a barren rock in the middle of the loch, looming forebodingly and mysteriously and above all, bloody difficult to get to.

"Does it look a little...*strange* to ye?" Nicola Oliphant asked, her head cocked to one side as her horse sidestepped impatiently.

Her older sister perched on her own mare, and instead of looking at the nunnery, kept her attention on the people of the little village which perched along the shores of the loch. "No' really," Coira replied, in that no-nonsense way of hers. "Just difficult to get to."

"That's what I meant."

Finally, Coira gave the distant tower the attention it deserved. "'Tis impregnatable."

"They're nuns." Nicola hid her smile. "I should *hope* they're impregnatable."

Her sister rolled her eyes. "I meant the castle. 'Twas obviously a castle, aye? Mayhaps some laird left it to the nuns in penance or some such. All I ken is I wouldnae want to lead the force who had to attack that thing."

Coira Oliphant was the oldest of the laird's six daughters, and everyone who knew the Oliphants—although they were quite a few days' journey from home on this adventure—knew the laird wasn't the sharpest lance at the joust, and therefore his eldest managed most of the clan's affairs. Anyone who knew them *personally* knew that Coira—in her braies and tunic and the sword strapped to her waist—would absolutely be capable of commanding the force to attack a castle. Even one in the middle of a loch.

When Nicola shook her head, her horse side-stepped again. "I wouldnae want to lead the force which had to get food and supplies out there each sennight!"

"Mayhap the nuns plant food?"

"In a tower castle?" Nicola shook her head again, then took pity on her horse and clucked the poor thing into motion. "There'd be nae room. Come, let us determine how guests of the non-attacking variety gain entrance."

Coira might be the leader of the Oliphant sisters, and the one who was angriest about Da's ultimatum, but Nicola was the healer, and she had a job to do. One which involved getting out there to the nunnery sometime this year.

Eventually, they found a chatty woman in the marketplace who directed them and the four Oliphant warriors who rode with them down to the pier. Well, they *called* it a pier, but 'twas a series of pilings in the water, to which a series of increasingly dilapidated boats were tied.

"Well," Coira snorted, hooking her thumbs in her belt and rocking back on her heels, "I have nae worries about leaving ye in that fortress...but I cannae guarantee yer safety if ye insist on traveling in one of *those*."

Nicola was busy untying all her bundles and satchels, handing them to the youngest of their escort to deposit in one of the rowboats. "Shh! If ye anger the fishermen with yer insults, they'll likely drop me overboard on the way out to the nunnery."

"If they do, they'll have to contend with me. I promised Mother I'd get ye here safely."

Nicola kept her attention on her task, so she didn't have to pretend to care what Mother thought.

The older woman had been distraught when she'd learned Nicola had accepted the invitation from the convent for a visit. Despite what she'd told her mother, Nicola didn't particularly *want* to take holy vows…she just wanted a month away from home.

A month away from Mother's demands, and Da's mad schemes. Four of her younger sisters had married this summer, and Nicola knew everyone was eying her next.

But as she'd told her mother, she didn't *want* to marry; not because she liked the idea of becoming a Bride of Christ, but because she'd had enough of being at the beck and call of one person. Mother had treated her as her own personal emotional-support-blanket for years, and Nicola was tired of it.

At the convent of St. Dorcas the Ever Petulant, she'd have people to heal, people who needed her. Aye, she fully expected to be pulled in many directions at once, and was in fact looking forward to it. Anything was better than spending the rest of her life catering to *one* person.

"Good God, Nik, this weighs a ton." Coira was standing calf-deep in the water, helping to load some of the bags. "Did ye bring a grindstone?"

Sniffing dismissively, Nicola tossed her sister another bag. "Of course I did. I cannae trust the nuns to keep my scalpels sharp. And stop complaining. One would think ye've no' spent each morning out in the yard, practicing with the men."

Her sister groaned theatrically as she stowed another bag.

"*Practicing with the men?* Dinnae let Wyn or Robbie hear ye say that; they'll think ye mean something else entirely."

"Something involving dicks?" Nicola asked innocently.

The young warrior at their side made a choking sound.

"Aye, Nicola," growled Coira. "Get in the boat."

Pleased she'd managed to discompose her normally gruff sister out of her annoying habit of shortening everyone's names, Nicola held up her skirts around her knees and grimaced as the water soaked through her leather shoes.

They left their escort in the village, after Coira assured the men—most of whom cheerfully deferred to her when their commander, Doughall, wasn't around—that she could handle anything a bunch of nuns threw their way. The sisters sat in the stern of the boat as they were rowed out to the island.

Coira's booted toe tapped impatiently, and Nicola knew 'twas because her sister hated inactivity. "How do the nuns get supplies?" she snapped to the fisherman in front of them. "Dinnae tell me they ken how to fish!"

The man's large back was to the pair, but he turned just enough to grin over his shoulder at Coira. "Does a woman's arms stop working when she becomes a nun? She can still throw a fishing net, aye?" When Coira scoffed, the man chuckled. "My father's father grew up in the village, back when auld Laird Gunn lived there. When his son moved his seat west, the village just sort of became property of the convent. Depending on the Mother Superior, our lives are either peaceful or browbeaten."

"There are that many nuns in the convent?" Nicola ventured.

The man snorted. "Nay, nae more than a handful. But they trade off the title of Mother Superior, making it bloody difficult to remember who's turn it is."

The sisters exchanged a glance; Coira's surprised and Nicola's amused.

The convent of St. Dorcas the Ever Petulant was sounding stranger and stranger.

Mayhap the ideal place for a month's escape.

There was a quay on the near side of the island, so Nicola and Coira were able to scramble out of the boat without getting any damper. The fisherman happily handed up the satchels of Nicola's healing supplies, then waved as he shoved off once more.

"Coward," muttered Coira.

But Nicola had already turned to the imposing barbican. 'Twas indeed the entrance to a castle, or at least had once been. Now, the portcullis was rusted in the open position, the massive front gates looked as if they never closed, and a short, well-endowed woman was hurrying toward them. She was waving her arms, which—in the simple brown nun's frock— made her look a bit like a bird of prey.

Nicola stepped back instinctively, and only barely managed to keep from falling into the loch.

"Thank the Lord and St. Dorcas ye're here!" puffed the small woman as she skidded to a stop on the quay. "Ye're the Oliphant lass, aye? Ye sent word ye'd be here, and we've all been excited to welcome ye. Here, give me that one too!"

As she spoke, the woman—the nun—was collecting the bags and packages, hanging them from her shoulders and around her neck. Up close, Nicola could see that she wasn't just well-endowed, she was…she was…*remarkably* well endowed.

The woman's breasts were large enough, 'twas a miracle she didn't just topple forward. In fact, when the nun placed one of Nicola's satchels *atop* the shelf of her breasts, the healer held her breath, expecting just that.

But the nun was obviously quite used to navigating life with tits bigger than her head. *Each one* bigger than her head.

Ye're staring.

Nicola blinked and turned away, knowing she couldn't meet Coira's eyes, or she'd begin to giggle. "Aye." Her voice emerged as a squeak, so she cleared her throat and tried again. "Aye, I'm Lady Nicola. This is my sister, Coira. She's my escort."

Coira, of course, was wearing a huge grin. "Pleased to meet ye." Instead of bobbing a curtsey, like she'd been trained, the eldest Oliphant lass pumped the nun's arm, as if they were both men.

Nicola knew she was only doing it to test the nun's balance.

The woman, for her part, reacting with enthusiasm. "Welcome to St. Dorcas's! We're thrilled to have ye both, although yer letter said ye'd be leaving us, Lady Coira?"

"Aye, I'm only here long enough to ensure Nik's safe and sound" Coira was still pumping her hand. "I suppose ye can ensure that?"

"I suppose I can!" The nun finally managed to extract her hand from Coira's, and was waving it about. Perhaps to restore blood flow. "I'm the mother superior here."

Well, *that* caused both Nicola and Coira to startle.

The shorter woman shrugged sheepishly. "It's my turn this month."

"This…month?" Nicola repeated.

"Aye, we rotate, ye see. To determine which of us fits the role better. I confess 'tis no' my favorite, but I *am* rather good at making people do what I want. I dinnae ken why."

Coira, who was eyeing the woman's jiggling breasts, muttered, "I can guess."

"I'm Sister Mary Titania. That was my name, back home, ye ken." The woman was cheerful piling bags onto her shoulder again. "Titania McGee."

Coira made a little choking sound. "Titania McGee?"

"'Tis a auld Greek name, I've been told."

"Can I call ye Tits? Tits McG—"

"Please excuse my sister," blurted Nicola, reaching out to snatch back one of her satchels. "She likes to shorten everyone's names to make her life easier."

Sister Mary Titania chortled gleefully. "She's going to have her work cut out for her, then. Come along, I'll get ye settled, and Coira can decide how long she's going to stay with us."

As she followed them, Coira muttered, "I cannae decide if it'd be hilarious or a penance to stay any longer."

Likely both.

The nun kept up a convoluted litany of instructions and asides and gossip as she led them past the gardens and washing lines strung haphazardly from the outer walls, through the open portcullis and into what had once likely been a barracks. Now 'twas…well, Nicola supposed 'twas still a barracks, only a different kind.

"This is where the acolytes and the nuns sleep," called out Sister Mary Titania as she hustled them toward the stairs. "This month I have my own room abovestairs—best part of being Mother Superior—and ye shall as well. Of course, we've nae courtyard, which is bloody inconvenient, but nae one asked me."

As they huffed up the steps to the great hall—luckily, it appeared to still be used as such, although there were enough religious tapestries and crosses hanging around for Nicola to guess this is where the nuns heard Mass as well—Sister Mary Titania called over her shoulder to them.

"This is our version of the chapel. 'Tis also where we have our meals, which can be confusing at times. I swear, Sister Mary Influenza starts salivating every time we kneel for prayer. Which is, after all, better than Sister Mary Novella."

Nicola glanced at her sister to see if Coira was going to raise a brow at those names, but Coira was busy oogling a tapestry which showed the martyrdom of St. Stephen.

I dinnae ken there was that many arrows. But I suppose if one chooses to depict the man nude, one can fit a few more in various places.

Since their hostess was waiting, Nicola hurried across the hall. "Sister Mary…Novena, ye said?"

"Nay, Sister Mary Novella. 'Tis what we get for allowing these lasses to choose their own names upon taking vows. She's the one who willnae bend her knees. She says 'tis penance, but I'm no' convinced 'tisnae some sort of ague. She'll be coming to see ye tomorrow after Prime."

Prime? Damnation, they expected her to start her day right away, did they not?

"Doesnae bend her knees?" Nicola panted, climbing the next set of stairs to the upper tower floors. What kind of convent *was* this?

"Och, aye. We have our collection of strange plagues and odd ailments. Sister Mary Epiderma will be able to explain it all to ye. Sister."

An older woman stepped out of the shadow, where she'd been hidden so completely she wrenched a little gasp from Nicola's lips. The mother superior began to hand off some of the bags. As she took them, the older nun inclined her head regally.

"Welcome to t' convent of St. Dorcas t' Ever Petulant, milady. We are pleased ye're 'ere."

"Sister Mary Epiderma is in charge of our infirmary, but now ye're here to help her, I'm certain our patients will improve."

"I am no'," the older woman growled. "I 'ave sent for Fat'er T'eodolp'is to come administer last rites for Lady Ellen."

Last rites? Oh dear. Nicola hurried after the pair of them. "What ails the lady?"

"Naught a pep talk and some fresh air willnae cure," grumbled the well-endowed Mother Superior.

But the older nun snorted. "The lady gave birt' four mont's ago, and 'as been slowly weakening. I fear an infection. Our *Mot'er Superior*, in all 'er wisdom, believes it can be overcome with some positive t'inking and scented oils."

Such a strange accent, but the woman was unfailingly proper. Nicola trailed her into a large room which had been portioned into six sleeping areas, each surrounded by white curtains. There was a set of large doors on the opposite end of the room, which opened onto a balcony.

The room was cheery—there was even a vase of flowers by the single occupied bed—and had obviously once been the laird's chamber. Nicola handed her satchel to Coira and hurried toward the occupied bed. The curtains had been drawn back, and a petite woman reclined against the pillows, her skin sallow and her cheeks sunken.

Her eyes were closed, and Nicola had to listen closely to hear the woman's labored breathing.

"Lady Ellen, I presume?" she murmured.

To her surprise, the mother superior snorted. "Lady *Helen*. Sister Mary Epiderma just likes to drop her aitches. Makes her sound like a bloody Frenchmen, if ye ask me."

The older nun scowled. "I ken yer dislike of my 'oly vow, but I'll no' forsake it."

Coira propped one hip against one of the empty beds. "Ye dinnae say 'H' out of penance?"

"Many years ago, I vowed to St. Dorcas to save all my teet', and if she did, I would never say the letter 'H' again—*Oh fook!*" she gasped, slamming her hands over her mouth. "Look what ye made me do!" she mumbled accusingly.

Sister Mary Tits was just chortling happily.

The older nun crossed herself thrice, then hurried from the room mumbling novenas.

"Well, that's got rid of her," Mother Superior declared with a nod. "Aye, this is Lady Helen Macpherson, puir lass. Her bairn came four months back, and she's given up."

Frowning, Nicola leaned over the patient, noticing the way her lank brown hair had been brushed neatly, and the fact she was younger than Leanna, the youngest of the Oliphant sisters. "Puir lass, indeed," she murmured.

When she reached out to brush the hair away from the young woman's forehead, she was surprised to find it warmer than expected. "She has a fever?"

"Aye. She's lost the will to live."

Nicola straightened and shot the nun a stern look. "What is this, the dark ages? *Lost the will to live?*" She scoffed. "I'm a medical professional. A fever is an indication of an infection."

Sister Mary Titania nodded. "I'll get the scented oils."

"Och, Tits," called out Coira, "ye dinnae think she'd fight to live for her bairn?"

Nicola was already shaking her head. "If the bairn died during the birth, it likely exacerbated—"

"Died? Nay!" When the nun bounced happily, it did all sorts of frightening things to the front of her habit. "He's a fine lad, braw, full of energy. A set of lungs on him that—" She grinned and patted her own chest. "Well, let me just say I'm impressed. He's auld enough now to feed mush, thank Christ Jesus, since his mother wanted naught to do with him." She shot the unconscious lass a frown. "We've been soaking rags in goat's milk for him to suck on, but the goat's starting to go off her milk. Well, I say *we*, but mainly—"

St. Crystal's eardrums, the woman could natter! "Mother," interrupted Nicola firmly. "Ye're saying the bairn is alive and well? Where is he? Mayhaps we could try bringing him to her side, seeing if that'll rouse her."

She had some ideas what might be causing the young mother's fever, and none of them were good, not this far after the birth. Losing the will to live might *actually* be a problem in this instance. Mayhap sending for the priest for Last Rites wasn't a bad idea.

Seemingly unbothered by the interruption, Sister Mary Titania pointed helpfully out the large door toward the balcony. "'Twillnae work, we've tried it aready. Well, again, I say *we*—"

"Ye mean Sister Mary Epiderma," guessed Coira.

"Nay, I mean our other guest. Did I mention him? He's the other reason we've invited ye to the convent." When Nicola and Coira rounded on her, her grin turned sheepish. "Och, well, mayhap I dinnae mention him after all. 'Tis a warrior, braw and handsome he is. Wounded nearby, and brought to us for care."

"And ye gave him care of a *newborn*?" Nicola gaped.

The nun shrugged, setting off more seismic activity. "He volunteered. And despite his scars and the size of his arms—which make me wish I hadnae taken vows, let me tell ye!—he's as gentle as a lamb with the wee cherub. Aye, he's—"

Guessing the loquacious woman could continue for some time, Nicola brushed past her toward the door. There were more white curtains here—likely more for appearances than function—and they swayed welcomingly in the afternoon breeze.

Nicola gathered the material in one hand, the linen cool in her palm, as she peered out onto the balcony. There *was* a man there, sitting on a bench near the crenellations some distance away.

He was hunched forward, and she could see little of him, other than the fact he was dressed simply—in a plaid she didn't immediately recognize—and had golden hair tied back with a leather thong at the base of his neck.

And, as the nun had said, he was *quite* large.

He sat with one leg stretched out to the side, as if favoring it, and Nicola could hear him murmuring something. Was he holding the bairn?

The thought of a man this large, this imposing, cradling a helpless *bairn*…well, something deep inside her went all gooey, and she suspected 'twas her ovaries.

Damnation.

"That's yer other patient."

The whisper came from beside Nicola, at shoulder-height, which is how she knew 'twas Sister Mary Titania, and managed to keep from startling.

"He came to us with a broken arm, a sword wound in his hip, and a knock on the head which kept him insensible for a bit. We ken he's a warrior—the farmers who found him also found a bloody tremendous sword—and we assume he was attacked and left for dead. Thank St. Dorcas, he's stopped vomiting at every breeze, can get around fine. But he cannae remember who he is or why he was in our area."

Nicola nodded without drawing her attention from the warrior. "Aye, head wounds can do that," she murmured.

And mayhap he heard her.

Because at that moment, the warrior looked up. He looked up and met her eyes and grinned, and Nicola's knees went weak.

Oh fooking hell.

He had one eye. The other was covered by a leather patch, the injury old and doing naught to detract from his easy good looks. A lock of hair fell in front of his cheek, and he tucked it behind his ear with an easy movement, all while gently bouncing the swaddled bairn in the crook of his other elbow.

He was gorgeous.

And she knew who he was.

A golden-haired, one-eyed fallen angel? One who carried a mighty sword, and looked as if he was built to do the King's work?